Odafe Atogun was born in Nigeria, in the town of Lokoja, where the Rivers Niger and Benue meet. Now a full-time writer, he is married and lives in Abuja.

WAKE ME WHEN I'M GONE

A young widow, Ese lives in a village where the crops grow tall and the people are ruled over by a Chief on a white horse. She married for love, but now her husband is dead, leaving her with nothing but a market stall and a young son to feed. When the Chief knocks on Ese's door demanding that she marry again, as the laws of the land dictate she must, Ese is a fool once more. There is a high price for breaking the law, and an even greater cost for breaking the heart of a Chief . . .

Books by Odafe Atogun
Published by Ulverscroft:

TADUNO'S SONG

ODAFE ATOGUN

WAKE ME WHEN I'M GONE

Complete and Unabridged

ULVERSCROFT
Leicester

First published in Great Britain in 2017 by
Canongate Books Ltd
Edinburgh

First Large Print Edition
published 2018
by arrangement with
Canongate Books Ltd
Edinburgh

A catalogue record for this book is available
from the British Library.

ISBN 978–1–4448–3620–2

Published by
F. A. Thorpe (Publishing)
Anstey, Leicestershire

Set by Words & Graphics Ltd.
Anstey, Leicestershire
Printed and bound in Great Britain by
T. J. International Ltd., Padstow, Cornwall

This book is printed on acid-free paper

For Victoria

1

It was in the painting that I first saw myself as countless suitors had often described me. Before then I would frown at my face in a hand-held mirror, wondering what they saw that made me so beautiful in their eyes. In the painting I am tall and slim; my dark hair is brushed back into a neat bun; a slightly bemused expression spreads across my face, teasing my lips with a soft smile. It is however difficult to tell whether I am light, brown, or light-brown; the artist's pencil had caught me in many colours.

This was a long time ago, when we had not seen much of civilisation, and our daily existence was guided by ancient rules and traditions. At that time, no one knew that it was that painting that would change the destiny of so many, or that the face of a son who would be gifted to us smiled faintly in its background. We saw it merely as a beautiful painting. And then it was stolen from our village on a dark, rainy night. Only then did we come to realise its true importance — after the High Priest gave a chilling prophecy, warning us of a curse that would follow our village for many years.

* * *

I should start my story appropriately . . .

My name is Ese, pronounced *essay*. I come from a small village of about four hundred people, a thousand cattle and one white horse. A dirt road connected us to the world, and it was this that brought merchants from distant lands to our commercial centre known as Main Street.

Market-days were rowdy; thick dust rose in the air, and everyone drove a hard bargain. Because business was good, the merchants came often, and so the road became the key to the prosperity of our village, bringing new faces and things, and the promise of more to come.

* * *

At the height of the village's fortune, I took a stall on Main Street, where I sold vegetables. My husband Tanto had encouraged me. He was a big-time vegetable farmer, and he ensured that I got supply enough to meet the merchant's demand. As time passed and I received more and more orders, I began to nurse the ambition of acquiring a second stall. For a while, I was consumed by this prospect, but, shortly after my twenty-fourth birthday, a few months before the seventh of our only child Noah, my husband passed away.

It was on a market-day, a Friday. Gloom swept across Main Street as the news filtered in from the farms, from mouth to ear and mouth to ear. Somehow, I was the last to receive it, though it buzzed in sad whispers all around me. When it finally reached me, I collapsed in a heap, at first, too afraid to cry. And then the tears came in unstoppable waves of the blackest grief.

Main Street shut down business for the day. And the merchants returned to their lands with bowed heads. For many market days they did not return, knowing that the village would be immersed in mourning and that business would be slow.

My son and I wept inconsolably. On many days, Noah refused to eat or drink. Seeing his pitiful state, I managed to pull myself together, and for him, I found a reason to live again.

★　★　★

Slowly, a bit of normality returned to our lives, but I was too devastated to go back to business. I sold my stall for a paltry sum and set the money aside, and I took to staple farming on a smallholding that I had always maintained in our backyard.

Even though I thought about it, I could not muster the strength to go to my husband's farm to harvest the endless expanse of vegetables. He had died there, struck by the branch of an iroko tree. The neighbour who found him fled to spread the news. Afterwards, none of the villagers would go near the farm because they believed it to be cursed, so all the vegetables rotted away.

I pushed the farm out of my mind as best I could, yet the memory kept coming back to me, leaving me so lost and alone. I struggled on for Noah's sake, wishing I would wake up from my nightmare. In the privacy of my bedroom, I heard Tanto's voice, gentle as ever, professing his undying love for me, and my eyes would pour out my heart. I'd tell him how much I missed him, begging him to make everything right again.

At other times, fond memories of him lessened my grief. In moments like this, I could almost smell him near and felt his essence, and I tried to trap it all in my heart so I could live the moment with him again and again.

Not long after Tanto's death, some of the young men who had wooed me before I got married began to show interest in me again. Now that I had become a widow, they saw an opportunity to win my heart at last. But I did not allow them near me, so they greeted me from a distance each time they walked by and saw me working in our backyard. When not on the farm, I enjoyed a good amount of privacy as a result of the wall around our house; it shielded me from the prying eyes of men and of curious neighbours who wondered why I no longer worked the stall or my husband's farm.

As time passed, Noah began to play again, and I began to view the future with optimism. But I failed to envisage that the way I looked could create such problems for me, as it had in the days before I got married. Back then the Chief of our village had done everything in his power to win my heart. He would ride to my parents' house on his handsome white horse, promising me wealth in the land and more. I spurned him each time, repulsed by the idea of marrying a man old enough to be my father, who had passion only for gin and women and neglected his duties, key of which was to commune with the gods, through the priests, to ensure the prosperity of our village.

I was not yet sixteen at that time. The budding romance between Tanto and I was the talk of the village, and no amount of pressure from my parents could dissuade me. Eventually, against their wishes, Tanto and I were married, and the old Chief retreated sullenly from my life. For a while, he was not seen in public, but he soon went on the prowl again, riding on his horse to pursue and acquire any young girl that pleased his heart.

My parents and siblings were incensed. They vowed never to forgive me. They said I had brought them shame, that I had spoilt their chance of becoming affluent citizens, so they disowned me. Soon after, the Chief added Tanto's young aunt to his legion of wives, and, instigated by their new son-in-law, who promised to make them rich, Tanto's family disowned us too. And so we became a man and a woman with no family.

It was a very difficult time. On many nights I cried myself to sleep, with Tanto whispering comforting words to me. I could not imagine life without a family. Thankfully, Tanto had a good friend called Kpofe. He treated me like a sister, and he became our family. But soon after Noah's birth, he travelled to the city to pursue his fortune and would not return for a long time.

Noah's arrival brought us so much joy. The rain had poured incessantly for many days prior to his birth, and this was said to be a good sign. As if to affirm it, a missionary arrived in our village on the day he was born. It was the first time a missionary would visit us; and though he was black, not white, we were very much excited all the same. A great multitude came out to welcome him.

Many said that Noah was a special child. The missionary said so too, and we requested him to conduct the naming ceremony. Although it was the duty of the father to pick a child's name, we gave the honour to the missionary, and he picked the name *Noah*, which, he said, meant to *comfort*.

On the seventh day, the day of the christening, the omens were good — the weather was bright and sunny, and birds sang in the trees. The turnout was impressive, even though both our families were notably absent. We prepared a great feast for the guests, and it was the climax of a love story that warranted us a colourful mention in the village's folklore.

The missionary stayed in our village for three weeks, and, in that time, he taught us about a greater God who dwelled in heaven. He showed us the Bible to prove his point, and he taught us many things contrary to all that we had ever known about our existence. All of us, even the Chief and the shrine priests, were intrigued, although none believed him. He attempted to use his teaching to reconcile Tanto and I with our families, but they remained adamant, saying that the concept of forgiving such an act of disobedience — as we had committed — went against the laws of our land.

He spoke about meekness and turning the other cheek. Many wondered at his words. By the time he left our village, his teaching had stirred something in a few of us. And the rain, which had taken a lull during his stay, picked up in torrents soon after he left.

In time, the missionary's visit became a distant memory, and his God a mere fable. Meanwhile Noah grew big and strong. By the time he turned four, Tanto encouraged me to go into business, and so I began selling vegetables from his farm — tomatoes, cucumbers, cabbages, carrots, spinach and a few others that changed with the seasons.

*   *   *

Main Street divided our village into two unequal halves. The middle portion of this road was our commercial centre. Several wooden stalls were scattered over it, and it was a thing of great prestige to own one as a trader. My decision to give mine up after Tanto's death turned out to be of ruinous consequence for the village's commerce. The merchants returned after our period of mourning was over, and discovered that my stall had been taken over by another trader, who could not give them the quality of service I used to. As a result, the fortunes of the stalls' owners fell into a downward spiral and their businesses soon reached the verge of collapse. Left with no option, the merchants stopped coming to Main Street.

One day, the woman known as Chair-Lady paid me a visit. She was one of the traders on Main Street; and by virtue of owning the biggest stall, she was regarded as the head of our market. Without being told, I knew why she had come. I welcomed her and fetched her water in a small calabash. After she had drunk, she wasted no time getting to the purpose of her visit.

'Business is at its lowest ebb in our village,' she began, and spoke for several minutes. She wanted me to come back to Main Street. I remained silent for a few moments after she had finished. She waited eagerly for my response, and finally I found my voice.

'I'm so sorry that business is not going well, and I wish I could return.' A small sigh escaped me. 'But I'm still devastated with grief, and my son has been badly affected by the loss of his father. He needs me more now. Going back to business will not give me the chance to care for him as he deserves. Besides, if I were to return, how would I get the vegetables to meet the merchants' demands, seeing as my husband is no longer alive to supply them?'

'There are other vegetable farmers in the village,' Chair-Lady replied with some hope, 'they'd be glad to supply you.'

'But they already have other traders they supply,' I countered.

'I could get them to give you preference.' She said this with the authority of her office, trying to impress me with it.

'It could be difficult,' I said, looking away from her.

'Not if I talk to them. I'll make sure you always get regular supply, that way the merchants will be encouraged to come back.'

'The other traders could sell to the merchants just as well. The farmers could even sell directly to the merchants.' My voice was unyielding. 'What difference does it make?'

'It makes a lot of difference,' Chair-Lady replied anxiously. 'The merchants prefer to do business with you. And, I must say, you seem to be our good omen on Main Street. Without you, things are not the same. Please come back, Ese.'

A long moment passed. I shook my head slowly. 'I'm sorry, I can't,' I said, looking away from Chair-Lady. 'Maybe someday I will come back. Maybe. For now, my son is my priority. I wish I could gladden you with a more positive answer. Please understand.'

'Our village is facing economic ruin,' Chair-Lady said despondently.

I lowered my head. 'I really am sorry,' I managed to say.

*   *   *

Noah had been eavesdropping on our conversation. He came to take my hand after Chair-Lady left. 'Mother,' he said, 'you know, I'm not a child anymore. I can look after myself and you can go back to your business.' He smiled warmly at me.

I smiled back. He was big for his age, and it often amazed me that he spoke with the confidence of a much older child. 'Yes, I agree you're not a child anymore,' I said with a laugh. 'But don't forget, you're only just seven. You need me more than they need me at the market. And I'm glad that we are able to spend more time together now.'

We held hands in silence.

'I enjoy spending time with you, Mother,' Noah said, a distant look in his eyes. 'One day I will take over Pa's farm, and I will supply you with more vegetables than ever and you can go back to doing business with the merchants again.'

We had no school in the village, so none of us had any education. But I always prayed that we would have a school one day, and Noah would acquire knowledge, travel the world and pursue a great destiny. I wanted to tell him so. Instead, I smiled and drew him to me, and I kissed soft words into his hair.

We did not have much to do on the farm that morning, other than to sprinkle water on the tomatoes and peppers that were beginning to sprout. Noah insisted on undertaking this task by himself. 'Please take a rest, Mother,' he said to me. 'I can do it by myself. Let me do it, please.'

Since the death of his father, Noah had tried to take on more responsibility, as if to say, 'I'm no longer a child.' I knew how much it meant to him, so I allowed him to have his way. I showed him what to do and went into the kitchen to cook. Through a low window, I watched him for a while as he worked, and I could not help wondering where he got the strength from. Just like his father, I thought with a proud smile. Tanto had always helped me out with household chores, something other men never considered to do for their wives. I used to complain to him that he was spoiling me. He would laugh and say he wanted to spoil me more. Watching Noah work, I wished a miracle would bring him back to us.

★ ★ ★

Following Chair-Lady's unfruitful visit, the traders who owned stalls on Main Street blamed me for the collapse of their businesses, and they vowed never to forgive me.

In their bitterness, they spread hateful words against me, and I became very unpopular overnight. Nobody wanted to be connected to me. Main Street was the soul of our village; now, everyone blamed me for its fall and none cared to consider that I was still mourning the loss of my husband. Friends abandoned me. My neighbours, who had been very supportive at the time of Tanto's death, looked the other way when they saw me in the street. Pa Umoh and his wife Ma Umoh, who had often paid me visits in the evening, no longer did so. Duka, the young fisherman who lived a few doors away, stopped bringing me fish. And the young men who had wanted to woo me no longer walked past my house — not that I cared about this.

Mercifully, Noah did not suffer rebuff, and he did not seem to know that I had become an outcast in the village. My son had found happiness again — on our small farm and on the playground. This was all that mattered to me. I told myself that the future would take care of itself. I had hope.

But I had forgotten about the old Chief.

2

The village was often quiet during the day, at which time the men and grown children would have gone to the farms, the rivers and the forests. Most women, like me, owned a garden in their backyard, which kept them occupied at various times.

During harvest time, with the exception of market-days, the village often looked deserted because the women and children would have gone to help on the farms. Our market took place every five days, and each market-day was like a carnival, a day to wear our best clothes. Main Street assumed a party atmosphere; the more dust in the air the more interesting it was. In the evening, when business had closed, the sound of drums rolled through the village. We cooked our best food, and the men gathered under the trees to drink palm wine. Later at night, lovers met at quiet spots, exchanging gifts they had bought from the market.

That year, with my stall sold to another trader, I spent harvest time working everyday on our small farm, sometimes with Noah. The farm provided us with yam, potato, maize, cassava, and green vegetables and we had a barn, in which we stored our harvest. Noah was always eager to work, but I limited him to the small chores.

About five months had passed since Tanto's death. We were working on the farm one morning, when the old Chief rode into our lives.

We had started early, hoping to finish before the sun began to burn. We had been working for about an hour when the sound of hooves reached us. Looking up, we saw the white horse, with its gleaming mane like a blade of light in the distance. It was the only horse in the whole village, and we knew that the rider could only be the old Chief.

We concentrated on our work, to prevent him from intruding on our lives. But he was not a man to be dissuaded, and he soon brought his horse to rest on the edge of our farm. 'Keep working, don't look up,' I whispered to Noah.

For a few moments, we pretended that the Chief and his horse were not there. He coughed loudly to draw our attention. Getting no response, he raised his voice to announce his own presence. 'The Chief is present on this ground,' he said.

He was a powerful Chief, even if he was now almost a bent old man. His subjects were expected to accord him respect. I knew that the consequence for not doing so could be very grave.

I straightened up. 'Long live, the Chief,' I said in greeting with a curtsey.

Noah took a cue from me. He prostrated and said: 'Good morning, Chief.'

He was dressed in customary style, a long robe of many colours with a rope around his waist, which I had always found very funny, but not on that morning. He nodded at us, and without bothering to respond to our greeting, he beckoned us with a red horsetail in his hand, the emblem of his office. Then he waved it in the air to chase away the flies that clamoured around his face. The horse neighed and reared in protest, apparently disturbed by the flies also. The Chief kicked it to silence it. In the distance, a handful of kids had gathered.

'It's well over five months since the passing of your husband,' the Chief announced. 'I'm sure you know what tradition requires of you.'

I felt at a loss. 'What might that be, oh Chief?' I queried respectfully.

'You should know,' the Chief responded. 'You're a widow now, you're expected to know as a widow.'

'No, Chief, I don't,' I replied with a frown.

He permitted himself a faint smile. 'A

17

meeting will be convened at the palace in a few days. An invitation will be extended to you. You're expected to attend. Your rights and obligations as a widow will be spelt out to you then.'

He waved the horsetail in the air. And then he rode away.

We watched horse and rider disappear into the distance, several kids running and screaming after them. And then the whole world became still. I was too shocked by the sudden visit to think properly. I asked myself what it was that tradition required of me. How could I not know it? I could not think of any answer.

'What does he want?' Noah asked, breaking the silence that had enveloped us. 'Why did he come?'

I turned to him and managed a smile. He pressed close to me. 'Why did he come?' he asked again.

'I don't know, but it's nothing to worry about,' I replied, running my hand through his hair.

We returned to work without another word.

⋆ ⋆ ⋆

The invitation came two days later, delivered by a ragged palace guard with no shoes.

18

Across his shoulders, he carried a short stick — his staff of office. I thought he looked more like a herdsman than a royal guard.

Noah and I were working on the farm when he came. Like his master, he did not bother to observe the niceties of greeting. 'You're expected to be at the palace by noon tomorrow,' he announced crisply, then abruptly turned and left.

The next day I arrived at the palace, as directed, accompanied by Noah. The palace was a rambling compound comprising several large huts built of red clay. The wall around the compound was tall, and one could see the thatched roofs of the huts jutting into the sky. The main hut looked upon the street, with the wall framing it on either side, and it had an elevated balcony from which the Chief often addressed the village. A large crowd had already gathered when we got there. Commotion swelled, thick dust rose in the air. Everyone was chattering away, and I wondered what it was they were so excited about. I stayed on the fringe of the crowd, holding Noah by the hand. I did not put myself forward or attempt to announce my arrival. I had been told to attend, not to announce my presence on arrival. So I waited.

About twenty minutes later, a gong sounded, and absolute quiet fell. The

19

atmosphere became thick with anticipation as all eyes focused on the balcony. And then the Chief appeared, waving the red horsetail lazily in the air.

'The Chief is now present,' a royal guard announced.

'Long live the Chief,' the crowd roared in greeting, jostling with frantic energy, causing the dust in the air to get thicker.

The Chief climbed gingerly onto a tall handsomely-carved stool, from where he looked upon the crowd. His robe was more colourful than anything he had ever worn, and his belly folded over the rope around his waist. Behind him were the royal guards and on either side of him stood a number of lesser Chief's wearing colourful beads around their necks.

'This great meeting was convened by the Chief,' the guard continued, 'to read out the rights and obligations of Ese, who lost her husband months ago. She has become a widow.' He paused. 'And now the Chief will speak.'

'Long live, the Chief,' the crowd chorused again.

The Chief cleared his throat. He did not bother to enquire if I was in the gathering. He did not bother to summon me forward. He spoke from high up, going directly to the purpose of the meeting.

'People of our great village,' he began, 'Ese is now a widow, and in our tradition, a widow must remarry within six months or lose custody of her children.' He paused. 'In Ese's case, she has only one child, a boy. So if she fails to remarry as prescribed by our laws, she will lose custody of the boy to his eldest paternal uncle.' Again he paused, and he cleared his throat.

On the fringe of the crowd, I held on tightly to Noah's hand. I was finding it difficult to breathe. I felt I was in a bad dream. I wanted to scream in protest, but I was too stunned by the proceeding to utter a word.

The Chief continued.

'Ese's right is to remarry as prescribed by our laws. Her obligation is to give up the boy if she fails to do so. This is the purpose for which I convened this meeting. I thank you all for coming.'

The meeting was over.

The Chief climbed down from the stool, waving the horsetail. The crowd began to disperse. I tried to push through to the front, to make my case before the Chief. But it was as if I was swimming against the tide; my effort was useless. Fearing that Noah would be crushed, I began to retreat with the crowd and decided that I would visit the palace at another, more opportune, time, to lay my case before the Chief.

'It is very simple,' I told myself. Firstly, Noah was my son and there was no way anyone would take him away from me. Secondly, I could not remarry when I had not fallen in love with any man. Moreover, I was not aware of any such law warranting me to remarry within a specific time and never had I seen it enforced before. This was the case I would make before the Chief.

★ ★ ★

We walked hurriedly, isolated from everyone by a wall of dust. On getting home, I checked the calendar on the wall of our living room, which was roughly marked with charcoal, and I realised that Tanto had been gone about five months and two weeks. I had only two weeks left to comply with the law, or else my son would be taken into the custody of Jaja, his eldest paternal uncle. Jaja was a very mean man. A shiver ran through me at the thought of losing Noah to him.

'Mother, are they going to take me away from you?' Noah asked. 'Are you going to marry another man?'

I turned away from the calendar and held

my hand to him. 'No one will ever take you away from me, and I will not marry another man,' I reassured him.

'Yesterday I saw four boys,' he said, shuffling on his feet.

'Where did you see them?' I was curious.

'On the outskirts of the village,' he replied.

I released his hand and I bent down and glared into his face. 'Have I not warned you never to go that far?' I asked. 'Have I not?'

'I'm sorry, Mother,' he said, squeezing his face into a frown.

'You're sorry? Tell me, why did you go there?'

'My friends said we should go there to pluck mango.'

'Has mango become food for you? Don't I feed you well enough?'

He gazed up at me with imploring eyes, saying nothing.

'Answer me!' I snapped. Then I sighed and softened my voice. 'Look, I've warned you before; it's not safe for you to go that far. Stop allowing your friends to tell you where to go and what to do. You should have a mind of your own.'

He pushed out his lips. 'I'm sorry, Mother, I won't do it again,' he said and took my hand.

'I will be very angry with you next time, you know that?'

He nodded. 'I know, Mother,' he said. 'I will not make you angry.'

'So what boys did you see?' I asked, pulling a stool to sit down.

He sat next to me. 'The boys who live in the abandoned building on the outskirts,' he replied. 'They told me they have no parents. One of them is about my age, the others are a bit older. Mother, how come they don't have parents?'

'They're orphans, their parents are dead,' I replied warily.

'And how come they live on the outskirts and not in the village?'

'Well, it's either that they ran away from the homes of their relatives or that they were thrown out,' I replied.

'Why? Why would they run away from home or get thrown out to live in an abandoned building?' he asked in a sad voice.

I knew that the answer to his question would sadden him more. So I rose and pulled him up. 'Please stop worrying about the orphans,' I said. 'Let's go to the kitchen, I will make us something to eat.'

In the kitchen, busying myself noisily to discourage him from asking more questions, my mind became preoccupied with the

Chief's words. I imagined that he must have been drunk when he spoke at the gathering. How could he ever think of taking my son away from me or forcing me into marriage? A quiet, bitter laugh escaped me.

★ ★ ★

Noah pressed further after we had eaten. 'Mother, tell me more about the orphans,' he said to me.

I remained silent for a moment, and then I decided to tell him all that he needed to know. 'What is it you want to know about them?' I asked.

We were seated by the lantern. A moth circled, disappeared from view and then flickered back again.

'I want to know why they ran away from home,' he said, then reached out to slap the moth away.

'Don't worry about the moth,' I said quietly. 'It's playing with fire.'

A brief smiled passed across his face. He knew the consequence of playing with fire. When he was five he had stuck his finger in the lantern when I was not looking. He had screamed in pain, causing me to jump round in fear. He never tried it again.

'Why did they run away from home?' he

asked, looking expectantly at me.

I leaned back and fixed my eyes on the lantern. 'In the tradition of our village,' I began, 'young orphans are believed to be evil children responsible for their parents' deaths. By tradition, they're taken into care by their maternal family and are treated as taboo. They cannot eat with or play with other children, and they're made to work as slaves for their own family. Because they're treated very badly, some run away from home. In other instances, if the family they are living with suffer any misfortune, the orphans are blamed for it and they could be tortured and thrown out. Whatever the reason for them leaving, they end up in the abandoned building on the outskirts.'

'Will they live in the abandoned building forever?' he asked.

'They'd probably live there until they're a bit older, then travel and not come back. At one point or another, every orphan either runs away from home or gets thrown out. The abandoned building is the halfway house, from which they travel to distant destinations. To remain there is to live with rejection for life.'

'But those boys don't look evil to me,' he said, a frown on his face.

'As I said, tradition labelled them so.

They're innocent children merely unfortunate enough to have lost both parents at a tender age.'

'So they're not evil?'

'No, they're not evil. They're victims of an evil tradition. It has been like that for as long as anyone can remember.' A sigh escaped me.

He stayed silent with his hands in his lap. I could tell in his eyes that the revelations deeply saddened him, but they were truths he must know ultimately.

Suddenly, the moth hugged the lantern, flapping its wings in a vain struggle as it was singed to death. Noah sighed. I sighed, too. After he had gone to bed, I remained by the lantern for a long time, thinking.

★   ★   ★

The next day, I walked through the village, hoping to find someone with whom I could discuss my plight. The sun burnt fiercely, the thatched roofs could be heard cracking, as if on fire. The women and young girls were plaiting each other's hair under tree-shades, enervated by the heat and talking in low voices. Only a handful of children could be seen playing about, and they did so without passion. The men and older children who had gone to the farms, the rivers and the forests to work were not yet back. As soon as they returned, the village would be stirred awake by a frenzy of activities, and thick smoke would go up into the sky as the women prepared dinner.

Hostile faces glanced at me. I wondered if any of them might soften their hearts if I approached them, but I could not muster the courage to do so. I slowed my pace, hoping that someone would give me a kind smile, a sign to encourage me to talk to them. None did, so I trudged on wearily.

I came to Main Street. It was not market-day, so it was empty, and the sound of silence echoed around me. The stalls looked abandoned, the entire market desolate; not even the incandescent sun could brighten the mood. I got to the stall that used to be mine. I lingered in front of it. Somehow, it looked isolated from the others, and I suspected that the new owner must have shut it down. For a while I was overcome by memories, of the time, not long ago, when so many merchants came to our village to buy and sell. I shook my head. I wondered which market the merchants had moved on to.

I avoided the palace, sprawling in the distance. I could see some royal guards strolling lazily around its vicinity. The old Chief was probably in his inner chamber, resting in the company of one or more of his pretty young wives. And the horse was probably resting, too, inside the compound of the palace, waiting to take its master to pursue and acquire the next poor girl.

I took a long detour, scrutinizing the houses that I passed. They were all built of red mud and had tall thatched roofs, yet, each looked so different from the others. Soon, I could see my parents' house — still as I used to know it, one of the few houses, like mine, that had a wall around it. There was nobody nearby, nobody visible within. I stood at a distance to see if someone would come out. No one did. I moved on after a while, a deep loneliness weighing on my heart.

* * *

At about noon, the same barefooted guard who had visited to summon me to the palace came to deliver a message from the Chief. This time he came without his stick. Instead, he carried a red cockerel, whose feet were bound together with a white rope. I was in the living room with Noah when he came. Unlike the last time, he greeted me politely, but I did not bother to respond.

'What is it you want now? What is it?' I

asked petulantly. 'Can't you just leave us in peace?'

'It's in peace I come with a message from our Chief,' he said with a bow.

'And what message?' I asked with disinterest.

'The great Chief asked me to present this cock to you as an indication of his desire to make you one of his wives. By that, you will no longer be called a widow, and you will not lose custody of your son.'

For a moment I was too dumbfounded to say a word. Beside me, Noah sat quietly. I could feel his heart racing.

'You will go back to the Chief and tell him that he has two legs of his own, or maybe the four hooves of his horse, and I will not receive such an important message from a guard,' I spoke at last.

'The Chief cannot deliver the message himself.'

'And why not?' I asked.

'Because you are a common widow!' he cried. 'Tradition forbids the Chief to deliver a message like this to you himself. He is doing you a favour, you see.'

'Now go back to the Chief, and tell him that I don't need his favour.'

The guard shook his head. 'I cannot deliver such a message to the Chief,' he said. 'You're expected to accept the Chief's proposal and go back with me to the palace to formalise marriage arrangements.'

I clapped my hands and shook my head in disbelief. A quiet laughter escaped me. 'Now I must ask you to leave my house,' I said in a warning tone.

'You're expected to come with me to the palace,' the guard insisted.

'Okay, wait for me.'

The guard smiled.

I went to the backyard, Noah hot on my heels. 'What are you going to do, Mother?' he asked repeatedly. Getting no response from me, he began to cry.

I found a large stick, and I returned with it to the living room.

'I demand that you leave my house now!' I shouted at the guard.

'No, I cannot! You have to come with me,' he protested, taken aback.

I attacked him, jabbing him in the stomach with the stick. 'I say leave my house!'

He ran out, stumbling as he did so. And he fled as fast as his legs would carry him, glancing over his shoulders and struggling to hold on to the red cock.

To my surprise, Noah stopped crying and began to laugh. I laughed too. I drew him to me and wiped his tearstained face with my palm. I tried not to show the fear that had gripped me, knowing there would be consequences for my action.

★ ★ ★

Not long after, a town crier could be heard sounding a gong and repeating a short announcement. 'The great Chief requests the whole village to converge at the palace in three hours' time for a meeting,' he said. Other messengers went swiftly to the farms to announce it to the farmers; to the forests to notify the hunters; and to the rivers to inform the fishermen.

Just like the first time, a large crowd had already gathered by the time I arrived at the palace, and I stayed on the fringe, holding Noah by the hand.

Soon, the Chief came out to the balcony, and he took his seat on the tall stool. His guards and lesser Chief's took up position. He wasted no time going to the purpose of the meeting. 'People of our great village,' he began, 'not only is Ese a widow now, she has also become a thug.' He spoke the words with venom, and he paused to survey the crowd. 'Today, I sent one of my guards to deliver a message to her, and she attacked him with a dangerous weapon.'

A ripple went through the crowd. The Chief raised his horsetail for silence.

He continued, his voice rising with every word: 'From this moment, I pronounce that Ese should be treated as an outcast, until I say otherwise. But the boy must not be punished for his mother's sins, our laws forbid that. And if she fails to remarry as prescribed by law, she will lose custody of the boy.'

'No one can take my son from me!' I yelled from the back of the crowd. A few heads turned to look at me.

I was trembling with a mixed feeling of anger and fear. I could no longer listen to the Chief's words. I pulled Noah after me; we left the meeting and returned home. For the rest of the day we remained indoors, isolated even from the noises of the village that filtered into our home.

★ ★ ★

That night in bed, my mind whirred. I knew that the Chief had married some young widows in the past, but none had been forced to marry him, so the situation I found myself had never been known in the village before. Could it be that the law actually existed and I just did not know it? Would it get to the point where I would be forced to marry the Chief in order to keep my son? I shuddered at the prospect. I could not think of myself living in the palace; it was known to be a place of bitter rivalry between the Chief's wives. It was even believed to be cursed. This last thought caused me to sit up in bed, pulling the blanket tightly around me, my eyes hopelessly searching the darkness, as if for answers.

I had almost forgotten about the curse. All the widows the Chief had married had lost their children within one year of their moving into the palace. The first child who died was falsely accused of stealing a piece of meat and was beaten to death by the Chief's eldest wives. The others had died in mysterious circumstances, but most believed they were killed by the jealous wives, who feared that their own children would have to compete with the children of strangers for the Chief's attention. After the Chief's first few stepchildren had died, the priests were summoned to exorcise the palace of evil spirits, but the deaths only stopped when there were no children left alive to kill. And now I was expected to marry the Chief, and possibly lose my son regardless. I fell back on the bed in despair. Of what use was it marrying a man I loathed only to lose my beloved son anyway?

Footsteps encroached upon my thoughts in

the dark. An intruder was in the house! This knowledge caused me to freeze in fear for a moment. Then I sat up sharply, propelled by the fact that Noah slept alone in the opposite room and could be in danger. A wide corridor separated us. I had to get to his room to protect him. I pushed the blanket away and sprang out of bed. The footsteps kept approaching and they seemed to be searching their way in the dark, cautiously. I thought I should scream for help. No, I must get to Noah first.

My eyes had adjusted to the darkness of my bedroom. I inched towards the door, my heart beating violently. And then a small voice called out, 'Mother, I cannot sleep.'

I froze momentarily at the voice, and then relief washed through me. I opened the door eagerly. I could see his small silhouette in the dark corridor. Noah! I pulled him into my arms and carried him gratefully into my bedroom. I realised that the events of the day must have left him distraught. 'You will be okay here with me!' I whispered to him. 'You will be okay.'

As I watched him sleep beside me, I knew that there was no way I could let the Chief take him away from me. And I knew that there was no way I could go to live in the palace either.

3

Fortunately, I did not need to buy anything from Main Street in the days that followed, as no one would have sold it to me. I got all that Noah and I needed from our barn and farm, and I couldn't care less that the village's economy was in deepening recession.

I was consumed by fear. What would happen to my son if the law the Chief made reference to indeed existed? Again, it occurred to me that to keep Noah alive, I must not marry the Chief. But that would mean losing him to his uncle Jaja; this I could not bear. It occurred to me to run away with Noah in the middle of the night, but we had nowhere to go, and I knew that we would not go far before the Chief's guards caught up with us.

Going to my parents or my in-laws for help was out of the question. The Chief had given them acres of farmlands and countless labourers. They would only compound my woes in order to receive more favours from the Chief — more land allocation, more labourers to till their farms. They could even be appointed as lesser Chiefs, and that would attract a lot more benefits for them. I thought of turning to Chair-Lady. She had influence, but I wasn't sure if she would want to help me.

I felt helpless.

All I could do was pray. But to whom? To the gods of my land, who were obviously responsible for my predicament, or to the God who dwelled in heaven, of whom the missionary had preached?

Surely, the gods of my land would not answer my request — they were on the Chief's side. I had never really believed in the God of whom the missionary spoke. But pathetic as I was, it occurred to me that I was better off turning to him for help. There must be someone up there, I reasoned; after all, it was natural to look heavenward when one was in distress. So I looked up and I prayed. I prayed so hard that afternoon that tears came to my eyes. I prayed that the God in heaven would protect us from the Chief and the laws of our land.

Afterward, I went to check on Noah in his room. He was fast asleep. He looked so innocent and defenceless. I kissed him gently on the cheek, and vowed to protect him with my life. Carefully, I adjusted his head on the pillow, and then I went out to the backyard to do some work on the farm.

As I worked, I kept repeating my prayer subconsciously, until it became a sad song in my mouth. I raised my face to heaven. Surely, someone must be up there, someone more powerful than the gods of my village, who ruled the affairs of the universe. Surely, it cannot be just an empty vastness up there. Surely.

Somehow, I felt better. I went to take a bath after I had finished working. I was in the kitchen getting ready to prepare our evening meal when Noah awoke and joined me. He looked groggy with sleep.

'How are you, Mother?' He greeted me with a yawn.

'I'm fine. And how are you? Did you sleep well?'

'Yes, I did. But I had a dream,' he said, a small frown on his face.

'Come and sit down,' I said, patting a stool, 'and tell me your dream.'

He sat next to me. The frown on his face deepened. 'I cannot remember the dream,' he said.

'That means it's a good dream,' I said, smiling at him.

'You think so?'

'Good dreams are always difficult to remember, but bad ones are hard to forget,' I explained to him.

He frowned some more and said, 'I can remember a bit of the dream now!'

'What do you remember?'

'I remember building a house . . . .'

'A house?'

'Yes. After building the house, I went to look for the orphans I saw on the outskirts of the village.'

I frowned for a moment, then smiled. 'You see, because it was difficult for you to remember, it means that it is a good dream.'

'It was a very colourful house,' he continued.

'It means that you will build an orphanage one day . . . ' My voice trailed off.

'I'd love to build an orphanage one day! I'd love to build it for the boys I saw.' His voice had come alive.

'It's a good dream,' I said quietly, after a few moments.

'Thank you, Mother. I hope I dream it again.'

We fell into silence as I sat on a low stool and began to blend tomatoes and pepper on the grinding stone.

★ ★ ★

A few days later, while Noah was out playing, I found my way to the palace. The days were ticking by and I felt a desperate need to make my case before the Chief. No one greeted me as I went, and I greeted no one. I thought of passing through Main Street, but I decided against it.

I walked quickly, eager to reach the palace. I prayed that I would find favour before the Chief, but I did not feel hopeful. A number of men returning from the farms avoided me. Some women hissed and clapped their hands in anger. I did not care to look at any of them.

I was met by a single guard when I got to the palace. And I was surprised to see that he carried a sword instead of the usual short stick. I did not bother to greet him. 'I'm here to see the Chief,' I said to him.

'The Chief is not at home,' he replied, raising his voice and his sword.

Other guards promptly appeared, alerted by the voice of their colleague. They all carried swords. And it occurred to me that the Chief had increased his security because I was now considered to be a serious threat.

'I need to see the Chief,' I repeated.

'What does she want?' one of the other guards shouted.

'She wants to see the Chief,' the first guard replied. 'I told her the Chief is not here.'

'Yes, the Chief is not here,' the others replied in chorus.

'Where has he gone?'

'It's none of your business!'

'I have come to marry him,' I said, without thinking.

And then they all smiled and put their swords away.

'You should have said so,' the first guard said.

'Can I see him now?'

'Come with me, please.' He beckoned me to follow him.

'No, he has to come out to see me,' I said. 'He needs to give me a public welcome before I go into the palace.'

They all grinned sheepishly.

'Okay, I will go and announce your presence to the Chief,' said the first guard.

He went inside while the others lingered around, their swords sheathed by their waists. They were all smiling pleasantly.

The Chief appeared speedily. And he came towards me with outstretched arms. 'Welcome, my Queen,' he purred.

I could smell alcohol on his breath. I held up my hand to prevent him from enfolding me. 'Wait!' I said sharply. 'First, we need to talk.'

'Please come into the palace where we can

talk in comfort.' He waved his hand to usher me in.

'We have to talk here.'

'Okay, my Queen. What is it you want us to talk about?'

'I have come to tell you that no one should dare to take my son from me.'

'My Queen, no one will do that. Not now that you are my Queen. The boy will be treated as a prince here in the palace once you are married to me.'

'Yes, that's another thing I want to discuss with you. I have not fallen in love with you or any man, and so I cannot marry,' I said, emboldened by the knowledge that this was the only way to keep my son safe.

The Chief coughed violently and the guards, startled, promptly pulled out their swords, as if their master had come under a sudden attack.

'But you said you have come to marry me,' the Chief said in a croak.

'I have not come to marry you! I have come to tell you to leave me and my son alone. When I meet a man I love, I will marry that man. But I'm not going to marry you or anyone else because tradition requires me to do so.'

An exclamation of shock escaped the guards. 'Abomination!' one of them cried.

The Chief coughed again, holding a hand to his chest and doubling over. The guards quickly surrounded him, as if to protect him from the assault of my words. He waved his hand weakly at me. 'Send her away,' he said in a whisper.

I did not wait to be sent away. I turned and stormed away.

Noah was still out playing when I got home. I went into my room, and I crumpled on my bed and wept bitterly, tormented by the two unpleasant options before me.

★   ★   ★

I did not allow Noah to know what was going on. I prepared our evening meal, chatting lightly with him, and I managed to stay cheerful while we ate. But at the back of my mind was the encounter I had with the royal guards and the Chief earlier that day. I wondered what would follow.

Noah came to me before bedtime, in a solemn mood. I thought someone had said something to him, and I felt a tightening in my chest.

'Mother, remember the dream I had?' he said.

'Yes,' I replied.

'I'd love to build an orphanage one day, to

provide a good home for the boys I met on the outskirts.' He sat on my knee. 'Please will you help me to build it, Mother?'

'But you are too young to build an orphanage.'

'But I'm not thinking of building it now. When I grow up, I mean.'

'By the time you grow up the orphans you came across will be adults, and they won't need an orphanage anymore.'

He remained thoughtful for a moment. 'But there might be other young orphans then, you see. I would love to provide a home for them. Mother, will you help me, please?' He took my hand imploringly.

'If that's what you want, yes, I'll help you, my son,' I said and smiled.

He jumped up with a scream of delight. 'Thank you, Mother!'

'It's time to go to bed now,' I said sternly. 'We have work to do on the farm tomorrow.'

'Yes, Mother.'

I led him to his room and watched him climb into bed.

'Good night, my son.'

'Good night, Mother.'

He closed his eyes and I left the room carrying the lantern.

★   ★   ★

I found it difficult to sleep that night.

A new day was beginning to break when I finally closed my eyes, and I was fast asleep when Noah came to knock on my door. 'Time to get to work, Mother,' his voice seemed to come to me from a far place.

I rubbed sleep out of my eyes and climbed out of bed. Noah greeted me with a hug. 'We're getting late for work,' he said.

'Give me a little while to get ready,' I said.

About thirty minutes later, we went out to our farm in the backyard.

It was almost noon by the time we finished working and went inside for food and rest.

I was in the kitchen preparing lunch when a loud knock came on our door. Noah rushed to see who was there.

'Come back, don't open the door,' I shouted and went after him.

But he had already done so by the time I got there.

Standing outside were five smallish men, who wore colourful beads around their necks. Their heads were bald and shiny, and they looked solemn, like creatures about to be sacrificed to the gods. Each had a fan of feathers in his hand. I knew them, but they stared blankly at me, as if I was a stranger. 'We are the priests of the land,' one of them spoke, 'and I'm the High Priest. We act in the capacity of Judges, and it's our duty to pass judgements.'

I was tempted to shut the door against them, but I knew that they must have come for an important reason. 'And what judgements have you come to pass?' I asked, holding his eyes fearlessly.

'We have not come to pass any judgement now, but to give you notice of the judgement we will pass in five days' time.'

'And what is this judgement?' I asked.

'We will not come to pass judgement if you get married within the next five days. But if you fail to do so, the judgement shall be that your son can no longer remain in your custody.'

It was all like a bad dream to me. Noah began to cry.

'As Judges, you are supposed to be fair men,' I said.

'Yes, we are fair men.'

'And you are supposed to protect the rights of the helpless.'

'No, as Judges, we protect the laws of the gods of our land.'

'What justice is there in protecting evil laws?'

'We have simply come to perform our duty. We shall come back if the need demands.' The five men turned as one and walked away.

Noah was crying loudly now. I locked the door and pulled him to me. 'We'll leave tonight,' I whispered to him. 'We'll go to a place where they can never find us. Where nobody can ever take you away from me. Don't cry, please.'

But he only cried louder, holding tightly on to me. I raised my face up to heaven. It seemed to me that all that was up there was an empty vastness. I broke down and wept with my son.

4

We gathered a few of our most precious belongings into two small bags in the dead of night, and we were ready to leave the village. When we stepped out of the house, a cold, dark wind blew angrily against us, as if to prevent us from escaping.

I carried both bags on my head, took Noah's hand, and we sneaked along in the dark. The whole world appeared to be asleep, only the wind and the chirp of insects disturbed the night. I had instructed Noah to walk quietly, but he was soon dragging his feet behind me.

'Mother,' I heard him whisper.

'Shh', I whispered back to him, holding him firmly by the hand.

'Where are we going?' His voice was cold with fear.

'Shh,' I whispered again.

A handful of stars in the sky cast a weak glow that seemed to hide the houses we passed rather than illuminate them. All the houses were asleep, with no sign of lanterns. The silence that followed us was surreptitious. Above the silence the dark wind swallowed the sound of our feet as we walked along an uneven path that threatened to trip us at every step. And as we passed through Main Street, a small shiver ran through me. The stalls had taken ghostly forms, and I thought that many eyes were watching our progress. I increased my pace. 'Walk faster!' I whispered to Noah, pulling him after me. Soon, we left the market behind us, and we were on the road that led to the outer limits of the village.

'Where are we going, Mother?' Noah asked, beginning to pant for breath.

'Shh,' I whispered. I had not thought of where to go. I wanted us to get far away from the village, then I would think of the next step. 'We're going where no one can ever take you away from me,' I said.

'Can we take a rest?'

'Let's go a little further, then we can take a rest.'

As we neared the dwelling of the orphans, a faint light suddenly appeared far ahead of us. I stopped and pulled Noah to me. 'Be still!' I whispered to him.

We stayed rooted to the spot. Soon, I could make out dark figures walking in our direction, and I could hear their voices in the quiet night. I dropped to the ground and pulled Noah down with me. Leaving the bags by the roadside, we crawled behind a tree nearby. 'Don't say a word,' I whispered.

To my own ears, the sound of my laboured breathing had become as loud as a drum. I placed a hand on my chest, to supress the sound. Squinting into the darkness, I could make out three or four figures now, one bearing a lantern and leading the way, the others walking behind. They had gone past the tree behind which we were hiding when one of them stumbled over the bags and let out a loud exclamation.

'What happened?' someone shouted.

'Give me the light,' another said.

'See, bags!'

'Maybe they belong to the orphans.'

'Let's open them.'

'No! They might contain something dangerous.'

'They are ordinary bags. I say we open them.'

The men squatted around the bags.

And then Noah began to cry.

★ ★ ★

The men identified themselves as royal guards. They seized us and took us back to the village and brought us before the Chief, who had to be awakened from sleep.

Suddenly, there were bright lanterns and guards everywhere, as if the village had come under a state of emergency in the dead of that night.

'We found them in the outskirts, trying to escape from the village,' one of the guards explained to the Chief.

The Chief instructed that we should be kept under house arrest until the case against me was decided by the priests. 'Not for one second are you to take your eyes off them,' he warned. He did not bother to address me, and I saw no point trying to speak to him.

The guards took us back home and threw a security cordon around our compound. I took Noah into my room, where he promptly fell asleep. He looked so exhausted and my heart wept for him. I lay beside him on the bed, but I found sleep impossible. I blamed myself for our arrest. All I wanted to do was cry. Without making any sound, so as not to disturb Noah, I allowed my tears to roll freely, and I hid my face against the pillow.

'Mother,' I heard Noah calling to me in the morning, 'it is daybreak.' His voice seemed to tug at me.

I realised that I had fallen asleep on his bed at some point during the night. The sun of a

51

new day pierced the bedroom through the gaps in the curtains. I raised myself on one arm and threw the window open. Noah was sitting up in bed, his back against the wall, the blanket drawn up to his chin. He was looking at me with round eyes. For a moment, I was lost. And then it all came to me, and I felt myself choking with tears. We were trapped; there was no way out.

I drew Noah into my arms, hiding my face behind him so that he would not see my tears. We stayed like that until I got a grip on myself. And then I looked into his face and smiled hopefully at him.

'Good morning, Mother,' he mumbled.

'Good morning, my son,' I replied. 'Did you sleep well?'

'Yes, but I'm sorry that I cried last night.'

'Never mind,' I said, ruffling his hair. 'You must have been very tired.'

'What are they going to do to us now? Are we going to run away again?'

'Don't worry, in a few days, when this is all over we will go somewhere far away and live happily ever after.'

'Where is this place, Mother?'

'You'll see when we get there.' I smiled to brighten his mood.

★　★　★

The royal guards assigned to watch us would not allow Noah to go out to play. Our movement was limited to our compound and farm. Noah wanted to know why the guards were loitering outside and why he could not go out. I told him not to mind their presence, that in a few days he would be free to go out again. I made up my mind to do a deal with Chair-Lady. We needed each other. In return for going back to Main Street, she must get the Chief to relax the law. With her on my side, the law could be set aside temporarily. Hopefully, the merchants would come back and then I would take my time to escape with Noah. For now, I must buy time.

I spoke with one of the guards, requesting an audience with Chair-Lady.

'Why do you need to see her?' he asked.

'I want her to take an important message to the Chief,' I replied.

He looked uncertain.

'A while ago she visited me to discuss a serious matter that concerns the whole village,' I explained. 'If you tell her that I have good news for her, she will understand. I would have gone to see her myself, but as you yourself know, I'm under house arrest. And surely, the Chief's order does not prevent anyone from coming to visit me.'

'Okay, I'll get your message across to her,'

he said reluctantly and walked away.

'Thank you,' I said after him.

Chair-Lady came to see me that evening. She was cold and detached.

'Thank you for coming,' I said to her with a smile.

'Why have you asked to see me?'

'Last time you came I could not give you the news you wanted to hear. That's why I have requested to see you, to discuss the possibility of reviving Main Street.'

'Are you saying that you are willing to come back?'

'Yes, I'm willing to come back, if you are willing to use your office to help me,' I replied candidly.

'And in what way may I help you?'

'As you must be aware, the law requires me to remarry within a period of time or lose custody of my son. The Chief wants me to marry him, I don't want to. And the priests have notified me that they will come to pass judgement in a few days. I tried to escape from the village with my son, but the royal guards apprehended us, and we have been placed under house arrest since. I'm sure you're well aware of all this . . . I need your help. Please I need you to talk to the Chief and ask him to give me more time. Surely, it is in his power to do so. In return, I will come back to Main Street and help to revive the village's economy.'

'You have asked a very difficult thing,' Chair-Lady said with a sigh.

'Think of the benefits for the whole village if I return to Main Street.'

'I know, I know, but we are talking about the law. The priests are already involved. And once they are involved in a matter, not even the Chief can stop them from performing their duty. That law has always been there and you may not have been aware of it because no one has ever broken it before. You are the first, Ese. It will be difficult for me to defend that or to influence the Chief on the matter.'

'Surely, an exception can be made in my case, considering that I can help to salvage the village's economy and put us back on the map of the region. You could put this before them to make a case for me.'

'I'll see what I can do, but I'm not promising anything. If I were to give you my advice, I would say marry the Chief. It's no small privilege for any woman to be married to the Chief. You will never have to worry about anything again.'

'But I cannot marry the Chief. I cannot marry a man I don't love.' I shook my head.

'What has love got to do with marriage?' Chair-Lady asked, baffled. 'You do not marry because of love but because tradition requires you to be married. Tell me, how many marriages were contracted on the basis of love in the whole of this village? Certainly, not mine. I don't love my husband, yet I have been married to him for nearly thirty years.'

'When I married Tanto, I did so because I loved him.'

'But now he is dead. And the law of our land is clear.'

I took a deep breath. 'What about Noah?' I asked, studying Chair-Lady's face intently.

'What about him?' she asked, scrutinising my face in return.

'What will happen to him if I married the Chief and took him to live in the palace? All the widows the Chief has married have lost their children. They say the palace is cursed.'

Chair-Lady looked away from me, unable to say anything. I knew then, without any doubt, that I must not marry the Chief.

We lingered in tense silence.

'Chair-Lady, please help me. I know you can.'

'Well, I must go now,' she said, still not looking at me. 'I will come back to see you.' She rose to leave.

'Thank you,' I said, rising up too.

I saw her off to the door. I could see the guards outside with their swords.

That night, Noah came down with a fever
that left him very weak. I got some leaves
from the neem tree in the backyard and
boiled them in a large pot. I made him drink
a cup of the liquid — he took it reluctantly,
for it was very bitter. Then I poured the rest
in half a bucket of water and bathed him with
it. He stopped shivering afterwards, and his
temperature dropped a little, but he remained
weak. When I had managed to get him to eat
a little food, I tucked him into my bed and
watched over him until he fell asleep.

He slept deeply. Feeling anxious, I stayed
up all night and fell asleep just before dawn. I
must have slept for about an hour or two.
When I awoke, Noah was still sleeping. I
opened the window carefully to let in some
fresh air. Noah stirred and opened his eyes
slightly. He mumbled something, then closed
his eyes again and went back to sleep.

I went to the kitchen to prepare him a cup
of neem tea. When I returned to the bedroom
with the tea, his eyes were open. I sat next to
him and placed my palm against his cheek to
gauge his temperature. It seemed okay. 'Good
morning, my son. How're you feeling?' I
asked.

'Good morning, Mother. I feel a little

better,' he said, speaking with a slight drawl, 'but my tongue is heavy.' He sat up in bed.

I smiled at him. 'It's because you are just waking up. Here, I brought you a cup of neem tea. You will feel better once you've taken it.' I held the cup to him.

'It's too bitter. I don't like it.' He made a face.

'But it will help you to get well,' I said gently. 'Try it, it's good for you.' I took a sip from the cup before passing it to him. 'Come on, drink it in one go.'

He held the cup to his mouth, tilted his head backwards, and emptied the contents gradually.

'I'm proud of you!' I said, collecting the cup from him and ruffling his hair.

'It's so bitter.'

'It's the bitterness that will make you well.'

'I'll never fall ill again so I won't have to drink it again.' He shook his head.

I smiled at him. 'Yes, my son, you will never fall ill again.'

★ ★ ★

Noah enjoyed a good appetite that morning and I felt happy and grateful that he was getting better. But my happiness was cut short when Chair-Lady came to see me that afternoon. She would not come in, and she stood by the door to address me.

'I did my best,' she said with a small shrug, 'but the Chief insisted that the law must take its course. If you don't get married by the end of today, tomorrow you will lose your son. But the good news is that the Chief is still willing to marry you to save you from widowhood.' She smiled, as if to encourage me.

'My son will die if I marry the Chief and take him to live with me in the palace.' My voice was filled with anguish.

'You will bear other children,' Chair-Lady replied coldly. 'And who knows, your son may be lucky and thrive in the palace. It's a chance you should take.'

'No,' I whispered, shaking my head. 'No, I cannot take that chance!'

'You would prefer to lose him to Jaja, knowing how wicked a man he is?'

My eyes filled with tears. And soon they were rolling down.

'I wish you luck while you wait for love. But let me tell you, I don't know of any bachelor who will want to marry a widow as a first wife. Your best chance is to marry the Chief now.'

'This is no longer about love,' I said with frustration. 'This is about my son!'

Chair-Lady sighed and shook her head, looking upon me with pity. 'I wish you luck. I must get going now. Goodbye, Ese.'

I watched her leave.

I made frantic efforts to reach out to my neighbours. I begged one of the guards to take word to Pa Umoh and Ma Umoh, but he came back to say that they were not available. Then I send word to Duka — he too was not available. With my heart beating fearfully, it occurred to me that my son and I were all on our own.

★ ★ ★

I went through the rest of the day in a daze. Each time I looked through the window, it seemed to me that the guards had increased in number, and that their swords had become longer.

I tried to get word to my parents, but the guards had become very hostile and they declined my request. I pleaded with them, but they pushed me back into the house.

All I could do was cry quietly while Noah slept. I lay beside him, hiding my face against the pillow. For the first time since Tanto passed away, I felt that he had betrayed me by dying. I looked up to heaven, and it occurred to me that the missionary had sold us a lie that a greater God lived up there. I had never felt so bitter. But putting my arm around Noah, I felt reassured somehow, and I told myself that the missionary was right about one thing — Noah was truly my comfort.

I fell asleep with my arm around him. As if a spell of sleep had been cast upon us, we slept all day and all night. I awoke in the early hours of dawn, and I was alarmed at how high his temperature had risen. He was covered in sweat and he was shivering beneath the blanket. I shot out of bed and rushed into the kitchen. I lit the stove, filled a pot full of neem leaves with water, and put it on to boil.

When I returned to the bedroom with a cup of the herbal tea, Noah was still shivering, but his eyes were now open. I found a small spoon, and I raised him up gently and fed him the tea with the spoon. He made a face, but I managed to get him to finish the contents of the cup. And then I went back to the kitchen and poured some of the herbal potion into a bucket. Returning to the bedroom, I dipped a towel in the bucket, squeezed it and used it to mop his body gently.

Soon, he stopped shivering, and his breathing, which was laboured, slowly began to relax. 'Mother,' he called, reaching for my hand, 'are we still going away?'

'Rest, my son,' I said. 'When you are fully recovered we will talk about it.'

'Okay, Mother,' he replied and closed his eyes.

★ ★ ★

Having no one to turn to, I looked up to heaven once again and begged whoever dwelled there to help me. 'I need your help,' I said, 'please make my son well.' This became my mantra for the rest of the morning while Noah slept. I stayed by his side, fearing to leave him for a minute. The longer he slept, the more fervently I prayed. Much later, he woke up, ate, and went back to sleep.

The nightmare took a turn for the worse when a loud knock came on our door before noon. I jumped up with fright. Noah continued to sleep. And then the house shook to its foundation as the door was kicked open. I rushed into the living room, and there in front of me were some royal guards, followed by the priests. Behind the priests were four muscular men, bald-headed and bare-chested, with eyes that glowed with fire.

I crumpled to the floor. 'What do you want from us?' I wailed.

The High Priest spoke. His voice was crisp.

'We have found you guilty of refusing to remarry, as stipulated by the laws of our land,' he said. 'As such, you shall lose custody of your son until you comply with the law.'

The muscular men stepped forward. 'We are the enforcers, and we have come to administer the sentence,' one of them said. 'We have come to collect the boy. His father's brother is waiting outside to take custody of him. In due time, you will be allowed to pay him visits.'

'Please don't take my son from me. He's ill with fever, he's terribly weak . . . please.' I spoke in a rush. 'Please don't take him away from me, I beg you in the name of your gods.'

Two of the enforcers gripped me by either arm. I wailed and struggled to no effect. One went from room to room, and he came out carrying Noah with one hand. My son just stared sadly at me, too weak to speak. He had silent tears in his eyes. And as they took him away, the men held me in a vice grip that made it impossible for me to go to his rescue. All I could do was raise my voice to heaven. Noah turned to look at me just once more.

When they had all gone, I was left alone in a heap on the floor. I tore at my hair as I wept, racked with guilt for not being able to save my son.

5

Now, I lived in a trance, alone in the house. I was still under house arrest, not yet a free woman. They had said that in due course I would be allowed to visit Noah, but I did not know their definition of 'due course'.

'We will tell you when it is time,' one of the guards said. 'You cannot go out yet, but you are allowed to receive visitors.'

But no one cared to visit me. I wandered through the house. I felt very bitter against the Chief, the priests, the enforcers and the royal guards. I felt certain that I could kill the Chief if I had the opportunity. The days dragged, the nights were longer. One afternoon, looking through a window, I saw Duka passing by with a net of fish.

'Duka,' I called out to him, 'I need your help, please.'

He stopped for a minute, and he gave me a blank look. Then he continued on his way.

I felt very wretched that I was unable to protect my dear son and I thought it was pointless to continue to live without him. I wanted to take my own life. But I reminded myself that if I did that, Noah would become an orphan and could end up in the abandoned building on the outskirts of the village. So I pushed the thought far from my mind.

I prayed fervently for the due time when I could visit my son. I wondered if his fever had gone; I trembled at the thought that he may still be feeling unwell. What were they doing to him? How were they treating him? The pain was too raw for me to bear. I stayed endlessly by the window, watching people pass, hoping for a miracle. None of them cared to look in my direction, and I knew that they were following the Chief's instructions.

In spite of my misery, life carried on normally in the village. I felt so pained I could no longer cry. Sometimes, I managed to cook and eat a little, just enough to keep me strong, for I knew that I must stay alive for Noah's sake. I reasoned that compared to a life at the palace, Noah was in lesser danger in Jaja's house. I held on to this small consolation.

* * *

Many weeks passed. I had grown very confused and weary. I was asleep one afternoon when a knock came on my door. It was not as loud as the royal guards would knock. I awoke at the sound and remained in bed for a few moments. The knock came again. I got up and went to see who it was.

I froze for a moment when I opened the door. I could not believe my eyes, and I thought I must be in a dream. Standing in front of me was Kpofe, very colourfully dressed. He wore a big smile, but it instantly faded when he saw my state.

I screamed his name and flung myself into his arms, and I began to sob quietly. 'I'm so glad you came,' I kept saying over and over.

'What happened to you?' He sounded bewildered.

I continued to sob on his shoulder, unable to say a word.

'Where is Tanto?' he asked.

I was sobbing loudly now.

He steered me gently into the living room and sat me down. 'What's the matter? Where is Tanto? Where is Noah? What are the guards doing outside?'

He stood there in front of me, a look of confusion on his face. Getting no answer from me, he went outside to collect his bags. He dumped the bags in a corner of the living room and took a seat opposite me. For a moment, he just sat there. Then he arose and went from room to room, obviously searching for Tanto and Noah. He went out to the backyard, and when he came back, he spoke to me firmly but gently. 'Ese, please talk to me, where is Tanto? And where is Noah?'

I stared dumbly at him.

'Look, I have just arrived from the city and I came straight here. I haven't even been to my parents' house nor had the chance to catch up with any one. Talk to me, please.'

It occurred to me that Kpofe couldn't have known that his best friend was dead, for we had no means of sending a message to the city. Slowly, I shook my head. I knew no better way to break the news to him. 'Tanto is dead and Noah has been taken into his uncle Jaja's custody,' I blurted.

For a while he just stared at me. And then for a very long time we both sat there, sobbing like children.

★　★　★

It took Kpofe several days to accept that his friend was really gone. He came to visit me every morning and he would not go back to his parents' house until evening. I told him how Tanto had died on his farm. He wept bitterly that he was not there to save his dear friend. He felt very angry that Noah had been taken away from me. He had gone to pay Noah a visit, but Jaja would not let him see him. For days, we tried to figure out what to do. And then an idea finally occurred to him.

'I'll pay the Chief a visit today,' he said. 'I brought some bottles of imported whiskey from the city. I know he loves whiskey. I'll present him with two and promise him more on my next visit. Then I'll beg him to reinstate your custodial rights.'

'You think it will work?' I asked, breathing unevenly.

'I hope it works. Somehow, we have to get Noah back.'

So, he went to see the Chief. When he returned, he gave me a smile, but I could tell that he was not satisfied with the outcome of the visit.

'How did it go?' I asked anxiously.

'Take a seat,' he said, pointing to a chair.

He sat opposite me, then he took a deep breath.

'The visit was favourable,' he said, 'but not entirely.'

'What do you mean?' I was eager.

'The Chief promised to give my request some thought. He asked me to come back tomorrow, but I sense that he is determined to marry you.' Kpofe sighed.

'But I will not marry him!' I snapped.

'No, you will not. If he remains unyielding

when I go back, I'll think of what else to do. For now, let us remain positive. And let us be prayerful too. I have started attending Church in the city, and I have come to know that there truly is a greater God in heaven. He answers prayers.'

'So the missionary was right?'

'Yes, he was.'

'But why has this God not answered my prayers? I have prayed to him so many times, and not once has he answered.' There was bitterness in my voice.

'Because he is a long-suffering God.'

'But I'm the one suffering, not him! If he is a good God, he should not watch Noah and I suffer so much. He should not watch them take my son from me.'

Kpofe was silent for a moment. He nodded. 'I agree with you, and I think that way too sometimes, in the face of adversity, but we just have to keep praying and hoping for the best.' His voice was almost resigned.

A lengthy silence followed. I got up and touched his shoulder.

'And . . . ' he said and stopped, his eyes fixed on the floor.

'What?' I asked gently, looking down at him.

He looked up. 'When you pray to God, you must have faith to receive an answer,' he said.

'What if you have faith and you get no answer?'

'Then it means it is not God's will for you. His will always comes to pass. Whatever happens to us is his will and we must learn to accept it.'

'So, indeed, all we can do is keep praying and hoping . . . ' I said quietly.

'Yes,' he nodded.

A deep sigh escaped me.

* * *

When Kpofe returned from the palace the following day, he did not come with the news we were hoping for, but he had delightful news all the same. He wore a happy smile that lifted my spirit.

'You're no longer under house arrest, and you're now free to visit Noah!' he announced happily.

I digested Kpofe's words for a moment. And then, realising the truth of them, I fell upon Kpofe's shoulder and wept with joy. 'I don't know how to thank you,' I said to him.

'You don't have to. Let's go and see Noah,' he said with urgency.

We hurried out of the house. To my surprise, I discovered that the guards were gone. And I realised that I really was free at last! It was as if I had woken out of a nightmare.

I took a deep breath of freedom. I was a step closer to regaining custody of my son. All thanks to Kpofe, and to the God who dwelled in heaven, for it was him who brought Kpofe back from the city.

To our alarm, we were told that Noah was not home when we got to Jaja's house. 'Where has he gone? Can we wait for him?' I asked, overcome with raw anxiety.

'You cannot wait for him, he has gone to a distant farm with his uncle. Go and come back,' the eldest of Jaja's wives said.

'Gone to a distant farm?' I screamed. 'But he's not well. How can he go to a distant farm, a sick child who is not yet eight years old?'

'Look, don't come here and shout! Go back to your house!' the woman retorted. 'Do you expect the boy to be lying around the house doing nothing?'

'You look, if anything happens to my son, I will hold all of you and everyone in this house responsible,' I screamed.

Kpofe touched my arm. 'Let me handle this,' he said.

The other wives had gathered by now.

'We're going to wait for the boy,' Kpofe spoke in a measured voice. 'Ese has the

Chief's permission to visit her son. If you try to prevent us from waiting, I'll take a complaint to the Chief. And I'll make sure that all of you are punished.'

The women exchanged fearful looks. The news had obviously gotten round that Kpofe had presented the Chief with two very expensive bottles of imported whiskey, and that by that gesture he had become a man of influence at the palace. One by one the women vacated the room, leaving only the eldest wife, who stayed back in a moment of defiance. And then, she too, slipped out of the room.

★   ★   ★

We sat down to wait in the living room.

Hours later, they returned from the farm. They came into the compound through a back entrance — Noah, Jaja, and four older boys. Noah was carrying a heavy log of firewood. I was shocked to see such weight on my son's head. I jumped up and rushed out into the compound. 'Noah!' I screamed.

He flung the log of wood away when he saw me, and a smile of joy lit up his face. 'Mother!' he cried and ran into my arms. 'Have you come to take me home?' he asked.

I knelt before him, holding his face in my

hands. I noticed that he looked thin and tired. I showered him with loving kisses. 'My son!' I cried. 'Oh, my son!'

'Mother,' he said.

'How is your fever? Are you well now?' I asked, studying his face.

'Yes, I'm well now. My fever is gone.'

Meanwhile, Jaja had turned on his wives, demanding to know what I was doing in his house. The women argued amongst themselves, each blaming the other for my presence.

Noah and I just clung on to each other in a tight embrace.

'The Chief has granted Ese permission to visit her son. And that's why we are here,' Kpofe said to Jaja.

'You can't come to my house without my permission!' Jaja fumed.

'We do not need your permission to visit the boy,' Kpofe said. 'And if you insist on making life difficult for us, I'll lodge a complaint against you before the Chief.'

Obviously, Jaja too, knew that Kpofe had become a man of influence at the palace. 'Okay, you have seen the boy. Now you may leave,' he grumbled.

'We shall leave only after we have spent time with the boy,' Kpofe said to him. 'There's no restriction as to how long we can stay. And I suggest that you stop taking the boy to the farm. He's too young for that. I'm not against you engaging him in little chores around the house, but taking him to a distant farm is not acceptable.'

'Who are you to give me orders in my own house?'

'We shall see about that when we get to the palace,' Kpofe responded.

Jaja stormed off, kicking the dust and everything in his way. His wives and children stayed clear as he foamed in the mouth. Feeling powerless, he went into the living room, his voice reverberating through the compound as he spoke to himself.

★   ★   ★

Noah sat between Kpofe and me on a bench in a corner of the compound, while Jaja and his wives and children held a rowdy meeting in the living room. I held Noah's hand and just stared into his face. I could not believe that we were together again.

'How are you, Noah?' Kpofe said, smiling at him. 'You wouldn't know me.'

Noah studied his face and frowned. 'No, I have never seen you before.'

'This is uncle Kpofe,' I said. 'I have told you about him before. He and your father were best friends. He left for the city shortly after you were born. He lives in the city now and has only come on a visit to the village.'

'Can we go with Uncle Kpofe to the city? I don't like living here.' There was sadness in Noah's voice.

'I'll come and take you to the city one day,' Kpofe said, his voice sad too.

'Don't worry, my son,' I said, sitting up and ruffling his hair. 'Everything will be alright very soon. Do they feed you well here? What have you eaten today?'

'All I have had is pap. On the farm, we roasted yam, but Uncle Jaja ate it all and didn't give any to us. He does that all the time.'

What a wicked and greedy man, I thought, fuming with silent anger. 'Okay, I'll go back to our house now and prepare you something to eat, and I'll be back shortly,' I said to Noah. 'Uncle Kpofe will keep you company while I'm away and you two can catch up. What do you think?' I asked, turning to Kpofe.

'Sounds perfect,' Kpofe said.

I asked Noah what he wanted to eat, and I dashed off to prepare it.

★　★　★

Kpofe used his influence at the palace to make sure that Jaja no longer took Noah to the farm. And he warned that if Noah was ever mistreated again he would make a lengthy complaint to the Chief.

To consolidate his position at the palace, Kpofe gave the Chief one more bottle of whiskey, promising to bring more from the city soon. The news spread round the village, Kpofe grew in stature. But he could not exert his influence on the priests, who were dour and unapproachable. Unable to access the priests, he focused on building a close relationship with the Chief.

Every day I awoke before dawn, prepared breakfast, and went to visit Noah at the first light of day. We ate together and then I went home to prepare lunch and then dinner. Later, I stayed with him until he went to bed. Kpofe often joined us with cheering news — the friendship between him and the Chief was getting stronger, and he reassured me that, very soon, the Chief would instruct the priests to restore my custodial rights. I could not wait for that to happen. In the meantime, I felt very grateful that I could see my son again.

As the days passed, my daily visits unsettled Jaja's home, and he begged the Chief to let me take my son back. But the

Chief refused, saying that the law must be followed to the letter.

In spite of the Chief's position, Kpofe continued to give me hope. 'It's only a matter of time,' he would say with an encouraging smile.

6

Kpofe said he had found love in the city. He told me about his girlfriend Eliza, who worked in a garment factory. He had brought some of the clothes they made as gifts for Tanto, Noah and I. Kpofe had had to give Tanto's to a cousin of his who had always dreamed of going to the city but never made it.

Noah loved his colourful new shirt. I had taken it to him in Jaja's house, and he tried it on eagerly. It was his perfect size, and he thought it made him look like a city boy. 'Thank you, Uncle Kpofe,' he said. 'I will wear it when I'm going to the city.'

'When you come to the city, I will get you more beautiful clothes,' Kpofe said, smiling.

Noah had given me his shirt for safekeeping. 'Make sure it is very safe, Mother,' he said to me. So I kept it in the same box that I kept mine. The dress Kpofe gave me was beautiful, a yellow flower-patterned dress that reached my knees. The first time I wore it, Jaja's wives gathered to admire it enviously from afar. They knew that Kpofe had bought it for me, for such a dress was not found in our market. They whispered amongst themselves, they moved closer to inspect the dress. First, they tried to befriend me, and then they tried to befriend Kpofe, hoping to get gifts from him. We smiled easily at them.

'I have never seen such a beautiful dress,' one of them said.

'Yes, it is really beautiful,' I replied. 'Kpofe brought it from the city for me.' I added, 'He got a beautiful shirt for Noah, too.'

'Ah, he is such a generous man,' she said, shaking her head and smiling sweetly at Kpofe. 'Ah, such people are very hard to come by in our village.'

'Omame!' the eldest wife called out loudly to her, not comfortable with her attempt to befriend us. 'Come here!'

Knowing that they could get into trouble, the younger women dispersed in different directions, and the eldest wife could be heard berating them. 'Wait till our husband gets back, just wait,' she grumbled. 'Outsiders have come to take over our house and you are trying to befriend them, traitors that you are!'

Kpofe and I exchanged amused looks.

★ ★ ★

It was Noah's turn to use the bathroom to wash that morning. Jaja had gone to the farm with some of his children. The wives went about their chores, while Kpofe and I sat on a bench in a corner of the compound, out of their hearing, talking in low voices.

'Tell me about the city,' I said to Kpofe. Even though he had already told me so much, I was eager to hear more.

He smiled. 'The city is a difficult place,' he said quietly.

I was taken aback. 'But you told me it is a beautiful place.'

'Yes, it is a beautiful place, but also a difficult place. If I were to tell you about the difficult part you may no longer see it as such a beautiful place.' He wore a serious expression on his face and he gave a deep sigh. Then he turned to me and smiled.

'I'm shocked,' I said, frowning.

'Don't be,' he said, laughing. 'I will not tell you about the difficult part so that you will not change your mind about the city.'

'Maybe you should tell me,' I said thoughtfully. 'Tell me about it.'

He shrugged. 'One day, I had gone to look for a job in a big factory,' he began, 'but the guards on duty told me to go away. I told them that I needed a job to survive in the city; they told me to go back to my village, that the city was teeming with jobless people like me, who made life difficult for everybody.

I felt insulted, and I spoke angrily to the guards. Two of them came towards me and threatened to beat me if I did not leave. I left and wandered the city for several hours looking for a job. It took many months before I finally got one. The city is a difficult place when you have no job.'

I shook my head out of pity for him.

'But it was in the city that I found love,' he said, to brighten the mood. 'One day, Eliza and I will get married.'

'It is a beautiful thing to fall in love,' I said, after a brief silence.

'Yes, it is,' he said with a sad smile. 'I hope you find it again.'

'I hope so, too,' I said. I wished I could turn back the hands of time.

Noah came to join us. He had finished taking his bath and had rubbed so much Vaseline on his face I could not help laughing. 'Come,' I said, pulling him to me. And I wiped the excess Vaseline off his face with my palms.

★ ★ ★

Noah told us about life in Jaja's house.

It had been a very difficult experience for him. They woke him up before daylight, every day, and his first duty was to sweep the compound and the front of the house. Then he must fill three mighty clay pots with water drawn from the well in the centre of the compound. He and the other children had a quick breakfast of pap, sometimes with bean cake, if they were lucky. After that, he and the oldest male children, who were between the ages of eight and twelve, followed Jaja to the farm, where they worked until late afternoon, or early evening at times.

There was no such thing as lunch for the boys at the farm, although Jaja ate roasted yam to his fill. Fortunately, they had water to drink from the streams, and, Jaja allowed them to pluck mango and guava, which he shared with them. While the boys worked, he sat under a tree picking his teeth after he had eaten.

Noah was made to work with very little rest. He cultivated heaps, weeded the land, and planted and harvested every type of crops. I had taught him to be hard working, but the work they gave him was far beyond him. And he could not give any excuse; he must undertake all the work assigned to him.

'On this farm, you're not seven plus, you're ten plus,' Jaja would say to him. And so he made my son work like a mule.

The older boys — Loko and Luku, twelve

and ten years of age, born of the same mother, the second of Jaja's wives — were kind to Noah. They helped him out with his portion of farm-work, unknown to Jaja. And they made sure he got extra mangoes and guavas, knowing that he must be famished and exhausted form undertaking so much hard work.

Noah did not get along with Kela and Kolu — eight and nine — who were always trying to get him into trouble with Jaja on the farm, and with their respective mother at home. Loko was the oldest of Jaja's boys, and a carbon copy of his father, but his exact opposite by nature. He once said to Noah, 'My biggest regret is looking so much like my father.'

'But it doesn't change the fact that you are a good person,' Noah replied.

'It's the reason why I want to be a good person. I don't want to be like him.'

Luku bore no resemblance to his father. He would say, 'When I grow up, I will remain my father's opposite in every way.'

But the younger boys adored their father, and they aspired to be like him.

Once, Loko had given Kela a heavy knock on the head for calling Noah an orphan. 'He is not an orphan!' Loko snapped at Kela. 'Next time you call him an orphan you will see what I will do to you.'

Noah told Loko and Luku about the orphans he had encountered in the outskirts of the village. Loko said that they had met them a number of times. 'I hope to build a home for orphans one day,' Noah said.

'It could get you into trouble with the Chief,' Luku said, uncertainly.

'Somehow, I will find a way to do it,' Noah responded.

'I hope you succeed,' Loko said.

At night, when they were in bed, they spoke in whispers with Noah, asking him questions about Kpofe, and all that he had told him about the city.

'Uncle Kpofe is a big man in the city,' Noah told them.

'Really?' Luku said in amazement. 'I'd love to be like him one day.'

'He brought me a nice shirt from the city.'

'Ah, so you're now a city boy,' Loko said in admiration.

'Yes,' Noah said, proudly. 'And one day, I will join Uncle Kpofe in the city.'

'Please don't forget us when you get there.'

'No, I won't,' Noah promised. 'I'll make sure you come to join me in the city, so you can protect me from the bigger boys there.'

Luku tightened his fist to show his muscles.

'I'll protect you,' he said.

They sat in silence then, the moon pouring its light upon them through an open window, each dreaming about the distant city.

★ ★ ★

Noah's story saddened me, especially the bit where Kela had called him an orphan. 'You're not an orphan,' I had assured him. 'You have me and will always have me.'

'I know, Mother,' he had responded happily.

We took short walks outside the compound now and then, with Jaja's wives watching us like hawks. The Chief had warned me never to take Noah beyond that street. I knew that if I did, he would make sure that I got punished. He could even stop me from visiting my son, which would be devastating for both of us.

So when Noah begged me to take him home, I told him that the time had not come. I told him we would return before long, and then he could play with his friends again. And as I gave him these assurances, I prayed earnestly in my heart that the Chief would restore my rights soon.

★ ★ ★

The village was thrown into pandemonium early one morning, when a handful of town criers went round to announce that the Chief's horse was sick to the point of death. Renowned herbalists were invited, and they tried to cure the horse, to no avail. Believing that his precious horse was going to die, the Chief took ill also. The priests invoked the gods, and the herbalists dispensed all manner of herbs known to them, but the Chief and his horse remained in critical condition.

And then the Chief had a strange dream. In that dream, he saw a young child holding a device to which his heart and that of his horse were connected. The boy was sad, because he had been separated from his mother and all that he had ever known. He had no one to play with, and the device in his hand was all that he had. If he pressed the button on the device, the Chief and his horse would die. For a while, the boy fiddled dangerously with the device. And at the point when he was going to press the button, the Chief jumped awake.

All the wise men in the land were called upon to interpret the dream, and they all came up with the same interpretation. The Chief must repeal any extant law that separates mother and child, or else both he and his horse would die. The only such law that existed in the village was that which required widows to remarry or lose custody of their children.

Kpofe and I could not believe what was happening. It was as if the gods had finally chosen to take sides with us against the Chief. Or maybe it was the greater God that had taken control.

'Will the Chief and his horse die?' Noah asked, captivated by the buzz of excitement that had gripped the village.

Kpofe said with a laugh, 'You tell us, are they going to die?'

Noah looked at him, puzzled. 'I don't know,' he said with a shrug.

'Then I think we should just wait and see.' Kpofe laughed some more.

For days the Chief remained stubborn. But as his condition and that of his horse worsened, the priests warned him to act on the advice of the wise men. Eventually, the Chief repealed the law on his sickbed. The priests performed all the necessary rites to declare the law abolished. Now I was no longer compelled by law to remarry. And so I regained custody of my son at last!

Kpofe was very happy for us, but he felt sad that he must return to the city. We wept and begged him to stay, but we knew that he had to go, that his life was in the city now. So we took solace in the blessings his visit had brought us.

7

Kpofe was far away in the city now. We carried on quietly with our life in the village; and for many days, I refused to let Noah out of my sight. When he was not on the farm with me, I sat in front of the house to watch him play with his friends, warning him not to go beyond our street. The kids gave him a rousing welcome. They showed him many things, and told him of all that had happened while he was away. And they asked him many questions too, about life in his uncle Jaja's house.

As time passed, I relaxed my watch over him, and he began to venture a little farther with the other kids. On some nights, after we had eaten, he would recount stories of his adventures to me, with the lantern burning numinously in a corner. He said he had hooked up with Loko and Luku. Their relationship was thriving, but because the boys often went to a distant farm with their father, they seldom saw. Whenever they did, they had so much to talk about, and the boys wanted to know if he had any news from Kpofe.

Early one morning, several months after Kpofe had gone back to the city, the village woke up to the news that the Chief and his horse had regained their health. A feast that would last for a week commenced at the palace. And many went to eat and drink, and to dance to live music supplied by famous musicians.

On the second day of the feast, Chair-Lady led a colourful procession of female dancers through the village, singing songs of adoration to the gods, and praising the Chief, too, referring to him as the Chief of chiefs. I watched from a window, and I could see Noah and several children screaming and jumping with delight in the street as the procession passed. The excitement was thick; there was so much dust in the air, the like of which had never been experienced even on Main Street. More and more women joined the procession; soon, it became an endless train of rapturous celebrants, made almost invisible by dust.

In spite of the way I felt about the Chief, I smiled and laughed to myself. I watched the train until it was out of sight. And, with the dust gradually settling, I realised that Noah and all the kids had gone with the train.

I was happy that Noah was enjoying himself again. I felt certain that he would not go too far. I shrugged and went to the backyard to do some work. And as I worked, the distant voices of happy singers reminded me that the old Chief and his horse were alive. But gratefully, they were no longer a threat to me and my son. A faint smile touched my lips as I remembered Kpofe. I wondered what he was doing in the city at that moment. I thought of Eliza, the woman with whom he had found love. Somehow, I sensed that she must be a good woman. I felt very happy for Kpofe.

I had just finished preparing dinner when Noah returned, covered with dust from head to toe. I could not help laughing when I saw him. He laughed too and asked why I was laughing.

'What happened to you?' I asked. 'You're covered with dust.'

He frowned and rubbed his palm over his head and face. 'Oh!' he cried, staring at his palm. 'Everybody was singing and dancing, there was so much dust in the air.'

'Sounds like fun.'

'Yes, it was! You should have seen the scene when some male drummers joined in. Everyone went wild.'

'I can imagine,' I said with interest. Then I added, 'Dinner is ready. Go and take a bath, then come and let's eat.'

'Okay, Mother,' he replied and went into the compound, returning a little later.

He ate quietly. I could tell that he had something on his mind.

'What's bothering you?' I asked, after I had done the dishes and we were lounging in the living room.

'I saw them again today,' he said.

I sat up. 'You saw who?' I asked.

'The orphans,' he said, looking away from me.

'Don't tell me you went to the outskirts again.' I spoke in a measured voice, certain that he couldn't have flouted my instruction.

'No, I didn't. I saw them in the crowd. They came to collect remnants of food outside the palace. They chatted with me and asked when I would visit them again.'

'And what did you tell them?'

'I told them that I could not visit them because you have warned me not to go that far again. They became sad, and then they walked away from me.'

'You did the right thing by telling them the truth,' I said after a brief silence.

'Mother, why can't we invite them to visit us from time to time?'

'We can't,' I said sharply.

'Why not?'

'Because we could get into trouble with the

Chief if he found out.'

'He's a wicked Chief. I wish he had died!' he snapped.

'Don't talk like that!' I scolded him.

He got up and stalked off to his room.

For a while I just sat there, thinking about the plight of the orphans and wondering if I could take the risk to invite them without getting into trouble with the Chief.

Later, I went to check on Noah in his room. He was fast asleep.

* * *

For days, after the celebration had ended, the smell of dust lingered in the air. The village looked drained from all the excitement that had passed and it fell back to the tedium of sluggish commerce. Now the days were much longer, the sun burnt harsher, and the heat seemed to stretch the nights. I worked more on the farm and Noah went out more.

And then one day, it suddenly occurred to me that my son was growing and becoming more independent — he was almost eight now. For a while, this realisation both gladdened and saddened me. And then I accepted that it was a good thing. I thought that it was time for me to go back to Main Street. Although I had not heard from

Chair-Lady since she last visited me, I had no doubt that she would welcome me with open arms. I discussed my intention with Noah. He was excited about it, and he encouraged me to go back. But for days I could not summon the courage to reach out to Chair-Lady.

I was surprised when Duka visited me one afternoon, bringing me some fish. He smiled and begged me to accept them. I took the fish and invited him to take seat. As I studied his youthful face, I thought he looked much darker and a little leaner.

'How is Noah?' he asked.

'He's very well. He has gone out to play,' I told him.

'I'm glad that he's doing well.' He paused.

I stayed silent.

'You're a very strong woman,' he continued. 'The Chief turned the whole village against you, but you prevailed in the end. You're truly a strong woman. I'm glad that you stayed true to your heart. By so doing, you have succeeded in changing a bad law.'

'Thank you,' I said quietly.

'That afternoon you called out to me for help,' he said and looked away, 'I should have done something to help, but I didn't have the courage. You know the consequence of disobeying the Chief.'

'Of course, I do. Please don't blame yourself.' I gave him a kind smile.

We chatted for a while, and then he rose up to go. 'Let me know whenever you need more fish,' he said.

'Thank you for coming,' I said, and rose up, too. 'I really appreciate the fish.'

He nodded and left.

★　★　★

I saw Duka's visit as an omen. So I went to see Chair-Lady, and I told her that I was ready to return to Main Street. At first she could not believe it. And then, realising that I was serious, she screamed in delight and hugged me. And, leading me by the hand into the street, she announced to the world: 'Ese is coming back!'

She sang and danced through the village, holding my hand, compelling me to dance along with her. Other women joined us. Children ran all over the place, screaming with delight, even though they did not quite understand what was going on. Some boys took to acrobatic display, drawing wild applause and shouts of approval. The fanfare raised an incredible amount of dust. By the time the whole excitement died down, everyone was thoroughly exhausted.

I bought back my stall from the woman to whom I had sold it, and Chair-Lady instructed the farmers to ensure that I got a regular supply of vegetables. Message was taken to the merchants that I had returned. A few markets later, they showed up. Once more, they commiserated with me over the loss of my husband. I thanked them for their show of love, and I expressed my delight that they had come back to our market.

The merchants came with a young man called Toya. They said he was an artist, and he wore his shirt with the sleeves rolled up. As everyone milled about the market, buying and selling, Toya found a quiet spot and painted on a large board. When he finished, he presented the painting to the merchants and they showed it to all of us. Toya had taken artistic liberties, placing me in the centre of the painting while the market buzzed around me. There I was, tall and slim and beautiful; not light, brown or light-brown, a bemused expression on my face. I was used to seeing myself in a small mirror, but never had I seen myself as a whole, the way I was in Toya's painting, which he titled *Ese*.

Deep in the background, I noticed the indistinct face of a handsome man who bore an uncanny resemblance to Tanto, gazing with a faint smile, as if observing the rest of the scene. I wondered how Toya had managed to picture Tanto's face. I was overcome by memories, and for a few moments I felt sad.

Everyone admired Toya's work and wondered at my beauty; and all agreed that Toya was a god in human form. Never had we seen anyone who could bring people to life. Surprisingly, no one seemed to notice the handsome young man in the background, and I saw no need to point him out to them. I was the heart of the painting, and so the focus of all their attention.

The High Priest carved a special spot in the village shrine — naming it the Shrine of Toya — where anyone seeking artistic inspiration could go to meditate. And with my consent, the painting was kept there. Toya blessed the shrine with his presence and left with the merchants when the market closed for the day. All of us had contributed money to pay Toya for his work.

Market after market, Main Street was a hive of activity again, and the dust in the air was more than before. Our economy slowly picked up, putting us back on the map of the region. The merchants were happy, everyone was happy. But my family, my in-laws and the old Chief remained cold towards me.

* * *

Noah went with me to Main Street on market-days. He gave me a hand with bits and pieces before running off to play. He came back whenever he was hungry, and soon after eating, he took off again. I had gotten him a ball from a young merchant called Bisco, who often boasted of his journeys to the big city. Football became a passion for Noah and his friends. Soon, a few other children got balls of their own, and soccer became a popular sport in our village. They played it without rules. The dust they raised on the playground was more than that of Main Street.

My neighbours became friendly towards me again. Chair-Lady was now a regular visitor to my house, and some of our traders' union meetings took place in my compound.

'I'd like to groom you as my successor,' Chair-Lady told me. 'I'm sure that when you take over, Main Street will become more prosperous than ever.'

'I'll do my best,' I said with modesty.

'I can begin to plan my retirement,' she said and laughed.

'No, no, not so soon,' I told her. 'You still have many more years at the helm yet.'

'We shall see.'

Prior to each market-day, I would spend so much time negotiating and coordinating deliveries from the farmers. I was busier than ever before, but gratefully, it did not affect Noah negatively. Instead, it gave him the opportunity to do his own thing with his friends. He was becoming a legend on the football field. Bisco had introduced some football rules to them. Now they played on a field with a goalpost at each end. Noah told me he was a striker, that he was a menace to many defenders. On the few occasions that I went to watch him play, I was astounded by his mastery of the game.

One evening, he came home sad. I asked him why, and he told me that the orphans who lived on the outskirts had wanted to play football with them but his friends would not allow them. He had pleaded on their behalf, but his pleas fell on deaf ears. And so the orphans left.

'If Loko and Luku were there, they would have supported me, and maybe the boys would have been able to play with us. But they were not there, and no one supported me.'

'Don't let it upset you,' I consoled him. 'Maybe one day they will be able to play with you.'

'Mother, please let's build an orphanage for them in our backyard,' Noah said, suddenly coming alive. 'We have so much space there. If they live in the village, they will be able to play with us. Please, Mother.'

'It's not so easy. And we don't have the money,' I told him. 'Be patient, one day things will change.'

* * *

The legend of 'Ese', the painting in the Shrine of Toya, travelled far and wide, and many handsome young men came to our village to admire it, and to see me in the flesh. They came on every day of the week and were all entranced by my beauty. Now I had to contend with a distraction — that of suitors ready to go to the ends of the world to win my hand in marriage. But I did not find any man among them that I could love, for they all loved me for my beauty, as a possession, and not for my heart. They were no better than the Chief.

Seeing the endless number of young men that trooped to the shrine, the High Priest levied a gate fee, and the takings made our village richer than other villages in the region. The Chief became a regular visitor at the shrine too. He would sit there for hours admiring me in the painting. Each time he went, he shut out the young men who came from afar and had paid to view the painting.

He was jealous and feared that one of the men could win my heart and end any chance he had of having me as his wife. His visits to the shrine created endless queues so that the young men who came sometimes had to wait for days to get the opportunity to view the painting.

Piqued by what they described as the utter insensitivity of the Chief, the men went on a protest that disrupted activity in the village for days. Thereafter, the Chief was forced to view the painting alongside everyone else. He was not happy about it, but the High Priest made it clear that the shrine could not afford to be embroiled in controversy.

And then one day, it was announced that the painting had been stolen.

* * *

Everyone knew that the Chief had stolen the painting, but no one could confront him. The young men stopped coming to the shrine. Our tourism industry completely collapsed, and this even affected business on Main Street. Many of the villagers were angry with the Chief. Chair-Lady wanted to organise a mass protest to demand the return of the stolen artwork. I told her that it was pointless, that the Chief would never own up to his crime.

The merchants said that they would bring Toya back to redo the painting, but all their efforts failed. He said that he never did the same painting twice, even if he was offered all the money in the world. And he said that the painting would show up one day, that every stolen painting was eventually found. Until then, we had to wait.

With our income from the shrine completely gone, Main Street became the focus for everyone. Occasionally, new merchants showed up, bringing things that we had never seen or traded before. They brought silver cups, and they brought torchlights and transistor radios that used Tiger batteries. With the coming of these things, our village began to connect a little more with the world.

★ ★ ★

I started to notice that Noah kept his room tidier; that he carried out his chores without supervision, and was often eager to help out with some of mine. And then he started returning home from the playground in a quiet mood every evening, and I could not help wondering what was bothering him. I made up my mind to have a chat with him.

One day, he came home particularly late,

and in a sober mood. After he had taken a bath and eaten, we sat in the living room, with the lantern burning in the corner, and I fixed my eyes upon him.

'Why are you looking at me like that, Mother,' he asked and laughed.

'Because you have been returning home in a quiet mood of late,' I replied. 'What is bothering you?'

He fell silent.

'I asked you a question,' I said to him gently.

He squeezed his face into a thoughtful frown, staring at me.

I raised my brow to encourage him to say something, but he continued to look at me. 'Say something,' I urged him.

'It's because of the orphans,' he said, finally. 'They have bought their own ball, but my friends still would not let them play with us.'

'Come, sit here,' I said, patting the bench on which I was seated. 'Is that why you have been coming home in a quiet mood?'

'Yes,' he replied. 'When my friends refused to let them play with us, I told them what you told me, that one day things will change. This made them happy and they told me about themselves. They told me how they run their home, how they share the chores amongst themselves, and how everyone did his bit correctly.

'They told me they have a farm, that they apportion farm-work according to each person's ability. I asked how they learnt to be so organised, and the eldest boy, Mofe, told me to go and see the ants, which having no leader, gather a rich harvest. I didn't understand what he meant, but I was inspired all the same, and I felt glad that they see each other as family.'

I held him close. It all made sense to me now. The orphans neglected by society had influenced my son positively. I knew I could no longer pretend that they were not a part of the village, and I made up my mind to encourage Noah to develop a friendship with them. It was a risk I was willing to take, if it meant that my son and the poor orphans would find happiness.

'It's sad nobody wants to play with them, and it's a good thing that you want to be their friend,' I told him. 'Next time, play with them. You don't need your friends' permission to do so. The orphans are your friends too.' My eyes were fixed on the lantern; the flame lit me with hope.

Noah pressed himself against me. 'Thank you, Mother,' he mumbled.

I patted him on the back. 'You have made

me so proud and given me so much joy,' I said to him. 'Just be careful.'

'I will be careful, Mother.'

I could sense a happy smile spreading across his face.

After a moment of silence, he said, 'Mother, could you tell me about the ants who have no leader but gather a rich harvest?'

'Yes,' I said. I told him about how ants live in a colony that has inspired the human race for thousands of years. I explained that the ant colony is made up of a queen, workers, soldiers, and so on, each with a specific duty which they undertake unsupervised, a model that humans have long been aspiring to achieve.

His eyes grew with interest as I spoke.

8

Suddenly, the season changed and the first rains came.

An angry storm tore through our village for three days, destroying entire swathes of farmland. It swept most of the harvests away, leaving us with nothing to sell. And it swept away all the stalls on Main Street. When the merchants came on the next market-day, they met a commercial centre in total ruin. Unable to undertake any trade, they returned to their lands greatly disappointed.

The wise men predicted that it was a season that would bring a terrible famine. They also predicted that commercial activity would be disrupted for a long time. As could be expected, the merchants did not bother to come back after what they had seen, and the village's economy slid into a recession worse than what we had seen before.

Farmers were advised to store as many crops as possible in preparation for the great famine to come. We no longer bothered to go to Main Street because we had little or nothing to sell and all our stalls had been destroyed. Anyone who wanted to buy or sell sought out those who wanted to do the same by visiting their homes — this became the mode of trading in the village.

After the first three days of heavy rain, the sun came out, but the scale of devastation we had suffered left a blanket of gloom over the village. The priests consulted the gods to find out the cause of such rains. Days later, the High Priest relayed a disheartening message. He said that the gods were angry with the villagers, that more terrible rains would come. But he did not say what the gods were angry about.

We all gazed into the sky hopelessly.

★   ★   ★

The children in the village were not bothered about the implication of so much rain. They prayed for it to stop only so that they could go out to play, not because they feared that the crops would be washed away. So when the rain stopped after three days, and the sun came out, they rushed out into the streets with their balls and played in mud and pools of water.

The orphans came from the outskirts too. They came without their ball; it had burst. So Noah suggested that they play with his together. They were overjoyed. They ran about with Noah on a small pitch away from the other children, and Noah was surprised how well they played.

It was easy to tell how close the boys were, even as they competed fiercely for the ball. Mofe, who at ten years of age was the oldest among them, treated the others with brotherly affection. When he got the ball, he made sure that he passed it around evenly. Igalo, who was a year younger, was very competitive, but he knew when to pull back from a tackle that could hurt any of the others. Tega, who was eight, and Bomboi, seven, loved the fact that the older boys often let them score goals, even when they were not playing so well. On the pitch, they competed in harmony, and off it they were one big family. Noah was glad to see that they were happy, far happier than the orphans who still lived with their wicked relatives.

'My cousins, Loko and Luku, said they have met you,' Noah told them at half time.

'Oh, yes, we have met. But we haven't seen them in a long time,' Mofe said.

'It's because they always had to go to their father's farm. But now that no one is going to the farm again because of the flood, we should see them soon. When I lived with them I used to go with them to the farm.'

Noah told them why he was forcefully taken to live in Jaja's house, and of his sad experiences there. His story invoked memories for them, and each narrated the circumstances that had made them run away from their own relatives. Their stories were sad. Even worse, none of them had any recollection of their parents. Each had lost both parents when they were still too young to remember them or even to know how it had happened. They grew up not knowing what it meant to be loved, and they were constantly reminded that they were evil children, that they were responsible for their parents' deaths.

'The life we live now is far better than it was with our relatives,' Mofe said. 'Then, we had no family because we were not treated as such. But now, we have each other, we are each other's family.'

'I'm happy to hear that,' Noah said.

'And we are happy to have you as a friend.'

Noah reminded them: 'My mother said that one day things will change. I believe her, I believe that one day things will change.'

'Maybe that day is now,' Mofe said, smiling.

News spread through the village that Noah had become friends with the orphans. It reached the palace, but, strangely, the Chief took no action. Some began to worry that something was wrong with the Chief, and they would gather in clusters to talk about it, but only in whispers, knowing full well that the Chief remained very powerful no matter his condition and could punish them in any number of horrible ways.

★　★　★

The village was greeted with grave news when the High Priest suddenly took ill. Many herbalists attended to him, but none could save him. On his deathbed, he said that a young man, whose half obscured face was captured in the stolen painting, would return one day to be Chief. Until then, he said, our village would not know prosperity. And then he passed away leaving nothing but worry and confusion behind.

The whole village wailed, not so much for the loss of the High Priest but because of the terrible prophesy he had made. We gathered on Main Street — all the stalls were gone now — to discuss our predicament. But the old Chief was not concerned. He remained in his palace, refusing to come out, or to receive any visitors, not even the priests who had gone to see him hoping to discuss the appointment of a new High Priest.

To avoid leaving a vacuum which could worsen the plight of our village, the priests entered a conclave and they elected a new High Priest to direct our spiritual affairs. But the new High Priest was overwhelmed given that he could not see the Chief to discuss critical issues. After trying for several days to see the Chief with no result, he gave up.

Not long after, bandits in black came to the village late one night. They ransacked the palace and stole all the old Chief's prized possessions.

Early the following morning, there was great commotion in the palace. The priests and many villagers rushed there and pushed their way into the Chief's inner chamber. To the surprise of all, they found the Chief wailing and rolling on the floor, saying that he had lost the most precious thing in his life. But he would not say what it was.

Afterwards, he became a very bitter man, worse than he was before. He accused his wives of being witches. He chased them around the palace, flogging them with a horsewhip in drunken rage. He threatened to sell off his children because they were useless and said that he would set the entire village ablaze one day.

* * *

Now we lived in a constant state of fear, not knowing what would come. The old Chief would not come out of his palace or receive any visitors. He spent his time lamenting his loss. The priests were helpless. They had critical decisions to take, but they could not do so without the Chief's consent. By our tradition, the throne could only become vacant if the Chief died or if he abdicated. So, even though the Chief was not performing his duties, there was nothing we could do other than to pray that he would come to his senses.

Somehow, we knew that the stolen painting was connected to our woes and the Chief's strange condition. Some thought the painting had driven the Chief mad. Even the staff of the palace, who were supposed to be blindly loyal to the Chief, were beginning to get worried and had begun to whisper that he was mentally ill. Considering the seriousness of the situation, Chair-Lady paid me a visit and told me that we must act to save our village.

'What can we do when even the priests are not able to do anything?' I said with dejection.

'The priests may not be able to do anything, but we must take matters into our hands.'

'What do you suggest?' I asked.

She looked round the living room. 'Where is your son?' she asked.

'He is somewhere in the house,' I replied.

'Find him and send him out to play. We need to be able to talk privately'

I went in search of Noah. I found him in his room, lying on his bed. I had taught him to stop eavesdropping on people's conversation, and he had been very obedient. I told him to go out and play, then I went back to join Chair-Lady in the living room.

'First we have to find the stolen painting,' she spoke quietly. 'It is the root of all our problems and those of the Chief also.'

I remained silent for a few moments. I wanted to ask her if she was sure of what was saying, but I knew that it was true. 'How do we find it?' I asked.

'We have to solicit the cooperation of a key insider at the palace,' she said.

'Don't forget that they are trained to be loyal to the Chief. We could be betrayed, and you know what that means. The Chief could charge us with treason and have us executed. You know that he remains a very powerful man.' There was uncertainty in my voice.

'I know the right person to approach,' Chair-Lady said, confidently. 'The truth is even the palace staff are getting very worried about everything, so they will cooperate with us. As it stands, we have no Chief. If our neighbours rose up against us in war, we would be doomed. Don't forget, there is very little the priests can do without the Chief's direction. So we must act to save our village.' Her voice was firm.

'So what do you suggest we do?' I asked.

'I will pay one of the palace staff to search for the painting and retrieve it,' she said. 'I believe that painting is the solution.'

An uneasy silence followed her words, and for several moments we remained quiet.

'Are you sure about this?' I asked at last, fear in my voice.

'Don't worry, I will take care of it,' she reassured me.

Days later, Chair-Lady recruited a senior guard at the palace to search for the painting, promising him a handsome reward. He searched for weeks, but never found it. He reported back to Chair-Lady that the painting was definitely not in the palace, and it seemed it must have been stolen by the bandits, for we all felt certain that it was the Chief who had taken it from the shrine. It was the reason why the Chief had been so heartbroken. We too felt terribly sad. We had no idea where the bandits had taken the painting or how to recover it.

'We just have to wait for the painting to show up,' I said to Chair-Lady.

'For how long?' she asked hopelessly.

'Toya said it would be found eventually. The High Priest also prophesised it before he died.' I sighed. 'We just have to wait.'

Chair-Lady stayed silent.

★　★　★

And then the rains came again, heavier than before, and it washed away all that was left of our farms. We all gazed up to the sky, somehow hoping that a sign would present itself to us, a sign of when the rains might end.

This time the rain fell for seven whole days. No one could go out. Noah became very agitated. He wanted to know why the rain was falling so hard. He asked if all the water in heaven was being drained. He said so much rain could only mean that soon there would be no water left in heaven, and then all of the earth would be washed away and heaven would be no more. I told him that the rain would soon stop and that the heaven and earth could never cease to be.

Luckily, our harvests remained safe in our barn — we were one of the lucky few. Whenever I was in the kitchen cooking, Noah worried endlessly about the orphans, saying that we should find a way to take food to them. But we were cooped up in the house — I promised him that once the rain stopped, we would take some food to them.

'I hope they have something to eat,' he said fearfully.

'I'm sure that they do,' I said, trying to alleviate his fears. 'They have a farm, remember? Like us, they will also have a barn, so they will have something to eat.'

'I'd love to start building the orphanage. Maybe when the rain stops?' he said.

'Don't worry too much. You will build the orphanage one day.'

An angry clap of thunder drowned his next words. We trembled and snuggled closer.

★   ★   ★

I told Noah folktales to keep the tedium at bay.

I told him of the lizard who fell from the tall iroko tree and praised himself when nobody would praise him. I told him of the parrot who fought her enemies and defeated them with incessant talking. And I told him of a time, long ago, when kings rode on golden horses.

The stories intrigued him. He asked me

many questions. He wanted to know if the kings in that long ago time were bad people like the chief of our village. I told him that the kings were good then, but that a time came when they had bad advisers who corrupted them and turned them into bad kings. And that was when wars began. Pestilence and diseases overtook the world. The tribes fought each other, and they invented weapons of war capable of wiping out entire villages. Hostility intensified and wars raged. Many people lost their family, many were displaced, and then a good king came who put an end to all wars. And then peace reigned.

'Are we going to see war in our village one day?' he asked fearfully.

'Our village has seen war before, a long time ago, before I was even born. So we are not likely to see war again because our ancestors taught us how bad it was. We know about the horrors of war, and we know that it could destroy all of mankind. We must avoid it if we want to enjoy prosperity.'

'Why do people go to war?' he asked.

'That's a question nobody has ever been able to answer, not even the great warriors. Maybe one day someone would find the answer. But we must pray never to see war again.'

The chill in the air bit harder, and we wrapped our blankets tighter around us.

After seven days, the rain stopped and the sun came out. We were not deceived. We knew that the rain would come again soon. But in the meantime, we hurried to do whatever we could while the sun lasted.

I went with Noah to the outskirts of the village to see his friends. It was the first time I would enter the abandoned building, and I was surprised to see how well the boys kept it. It was the first time for Noah, too. I could see in his eyes how impressed he was.

The boys were delighted to see us. Noah introduced them to me in turn. They, greeted me with warm hugs. I felt moved and I smiled at them and assured them that one day things would change.

We had taken some food with us, so I went to their kitchen and cooked yam pottage, using some of the smoked fish I got from Duka. We ate together, and they told me stories of their lives. They said they were much happier living there in the abandoned building than living with families who treated them worse than slaves. I promised that I would help them and that one day they would be treated with the love and compassion they deserved.

'How are you going to do that?' Tega asked, very much intrigued.

'I don't know yet,' I replied. 'But I will find a way. I will talk to Chair-Lady and try to appeal to her motherly instincts. I'm sure she will help me. And together we will take our petition to the Chief and the priests. Don't worry, somehow, I will find a way.'

'Thank you, Mother,' Noah said, beaming with pride.

'You're both very kind. Your son is like you.' Mofe's voice was quiet.

I wanted to say that Noah was like his father too, but I did not want to open a floodgate of memories. 'Thank you,' I said. And I asked Bomboi, the youngest boy, 'I hope your brothers are taking good care of you?'

'Yes, they are,' he said. 'But sometimes they don't let me score enough goals when we play football.'

We all laughed.

'Mother, can they visit us sometime?' Noah asked eagerly.

'Yes, you should visit us,' I told the boys. 'The Chief does not react to anything these days. I'm sure that he won't do anything even if he got to know.'

They screamed with excitement. I felt uplifted to see them so happy.

Igalo asked, 'What is wrong with the Chief?'

'I don't know. Nobody knows,' I said. 'But all is not well with him.'

None of them showed any emotion.

After we had eaten, they told me about the bandits who had lodged with them for a night, how the men had treated them so well. 'Come, come and see the room where they passed the night,' Bomboi said eagerly, pulling me by the hand and leading me into a room.

It was a large room filled with old stuff such as wooden boxes crammed with worn clothes, broken farm tools, compressed baskets, wooden boards and torn mats.

Mofe explained to me, 'This was where they spent the night. They drank and smoked cigarettes all night, talking loudly about their past adventures. And they gave us biscuits and sweet drinks, which they had stolen from the city. They told us they were not proud of themselves, that society made them what they are, and that was why they stole from the rich and gave to the poor. They said that they had grown up as orphans themselves in a faraway village. Before they left, they gave us some money and food. And they advised us not to follow a life of crime. They were very nice men,' he concluded.

I wanted to ask if they had seen a large painting with the men, but I knew there was no point.

We spent several happy hours together, then Noah and I had to leave for home to avoid the rain which threatened to start falling once again.

★ ★ ★

I spoke to Chair-Lady about the orphans when I next saw her.

'They could not possibly be evil children,' I told her. 'I paid them a visit with my son. They're very well-behaved and polite, even though they have no guardian.'

'You must be careful,' Chair-Lady said, a worried look on her face. 'If the Chief gets to know you could be in big trouble. What were you thinking going to visit those boys?'

'It's not their fault that they lost their parents,' I said. 'Is it possible that the gods are angry with us because of the way we treat orphans? Have you ever thought about it that way? That the rains are our punishments? These are hopeless children who should be treated with love, instead we neglect them. They could be our children. I wouldn't want my son to end up like them.'

'The priests say they are evil and should be

treated as such. They speak for the gods. What else is there to say? Look, Ese, I warn you again, if the Chief gets to know about this you could be in serious trouble.'

'Think of them as your children,' I pleaded. 'Imagine that something happened to you and your husband — not that I pray for that — and your children were treated as badly as those orphans. How would you feel? Those boys deserve to be loved.'

'Look, we should be thinking of how to revive our economy, not how to rehabilitate orphans,' she said. 'Leave matters of tradition to the priests and let's concentrate on how to restore Main Street. Take my advice, don't do anything that will get you into trouble with the Chief. You know what he's capable of.'

'Chair-Lady, . . . '

She cut me off. 'No buts!'

I felt disappointed by her response, but I was determined not to give up.

★   ★   ★

Word got to the palace sooner than I thought that my son and I had visited the orphans. But to the surprise of all, it did not elicit any response from the Chief. He felt too sad about his loss to bother with anything or anyone. He had stopped coming out of his inner chamber, and he would not see or speak with anyone, including his wives. They took his food to him. He ate alone, and left the dishes outside his door. At night, he could be heard wailing and cursing the bandits who had stolen his most treasured asset. His wives became very worried. Although they never cooperated amongst themselves, they saw the need to come together to address their common problem. They called a meeting and debated what to do. Each had a different idea, and the rowdy meeting ended in a brawl.

I saw the Chief's condition as an opportunity to give the orphans a treat in my house. The Chief was the only person who could take action against me. And as long as he remained in the condition that he was, I knew that I could get away with it. So I invited the orphans over and we had a feast. I had never seen Noah so happy. The orphans said it was the happiest day of their lives.

Chair-Lady showed up soon after they had left. Word had reached her. In fact, the whole village was agog with the news that the orphans had been in my house. 'Ese, Ese, Ese!' she cried. 'How many times did I call you?'

'Three times,' I replied.

'I won't call you a fourth time. I have come to give you a warning. Don't get yourself into trouble with the Chief. Don't allow those boys in your house again. I have said all I can. I only hope you will listen.' At that she turned and left.

9

Days later, news of the Chief's death spread round the village. We all rushed to the palace. When we had all gathered, the High Priest addressed us from the balcony of the palace. He explained that the Chief had locked himself in his bedroom for days. And when the servants took his breakfast to him that morning, they found him immobile on the floor with an empty bottle of whisky by his side. He had died of his drunkenness.

The gathering broke down in a loud cry. It was tradition for everyone to wail very loudly when a chief died, even if you were not pained at all by the death. Only the wives were not allowed to cry. They were locked up in a black room, all dressed in black, and they were fed with ashes to intensify their sorrow. They were to live in the black room for a whole month. And when a new Chief had been appointed, they would be married to him. This was the tradition of our village.

As required by tradition, I joined the gathering to wail, and I wailed until my lungs were bursting and there was no breath left in me. 'Ah, our Chief is dead,' I cried like everyone, putting my hands on my head. Many flogged themselves on the ground and tore their garments, like lunatics. I told myself that I would not go that far for the old Chief. In truth, mine were tears of joy for I knew that I was free at last from my tormentor.

The High priest encouraged us to cry louder. It was the way to show that we really loved our chief. Our tearful voices were supposed to accompany him to the other world, where the gods would receive him with fanfare seeing that he had served his subjects well and that they truly loved him. So everyone wailed louder. The High Priest kept motioning with his hands for more. Many began jumping up and beating their chests with venom. Everyone was watching everyone to see who was not crying loud enough. Such persons could be termed to be witches or wizards, and they could be lynched for being the cause of the Chief's death.

While we were yet crying, a huge commotion began on the balcony. The High Priest began to scream in fright. When we looked closely, we discovered that the Chief had come out to the balcony with a horsewhip, screaming and lashing at the High priest and the palace staff who were on the balcony, asking why the entire village had gathered to disturb his peaceful sleep.

The Chief had woken up from his drunken stupor, but we thought that he had woken up from the dead. Everyone took to their heels. The rain suddenly began to pour, chasing us to our homes.

After that, the Chief regained his senses and took charge of the village's affair again. He rode on his horse round the village, scowling at everyone to establish his authority. We all sensed that he would now rule the village with an iron fist, worse than before. I wondered if they would tell him all that had transpired while he had locked himself in his bedroom. I told myself that I must be careful. Chair-Lady had told me that she would not call me a fourth time. And by that she meant that she would not come to my rescue in the time of trouble.

★ ★ ★

Fortunately, the Chief did not take action against me. Instead, he kept sending servant after servant, asking me to marry him. The servants approached me on their knees. They told me that the Chief had instructed them to come before me on their knees, to show how much he wanted to have me as his wife. I sent them back on their knees, with the message that nothing had changed since the last time.

127

It was said that my message left him heartbroken.

I could not tell whether the Chief had enlisted the help of Chair-Lady to convince me to marry him. But she came to me, telling me that I was too young to remain a widow forever.

'Marry the Chief,' she told me. 'When you become his wife you can get him to pass laws that would be favourable to the orphans. You and I can work together to get a lot of things done in this village. Can't you see?'

'Chair-Lady, I said it before. I say it again, I cannot marry the Chief.' And then I added, to keep her on my side, 'I agree with you that we should be more concerned about reviving our economy. I'm prepared to work with you in that regard. It's far more important than anything else.'

I saw a brief smile on her face. 'True,' she said, 'our economy is far more important than anything else.' And she nodded her head.

★   ★   ★

The rain was falling more and more now, and we were trapped in our houses for longer periods. I noticed that Noah slept more, and when he was awake, he seemed to be drained of life. I thought it was the rain. I told him more stories to cheer him up. His eyes lit up with interest, but he remained very weak. And then late one evening I discovered that he was actually coming down with a fever.

I panicked, remembering the last time Noah had been ill, and how bad it was.

I boiled some neem leaves and got him to drink a cup of it and I bathed him with a bucket of the herbal potion. I prayed that he would be better in the morning. But when morning came his condition had deteriorated. His body was hot as coal, and he could not speak or get out of bed. He looked at me without life in his eyes. I broke down and wept.

But I told myself that crying would not do any good. I fed him more neem tea and I carried him out of bed and bathed him. I could not get him to eat anything. I prepared him his best dish, but he would not touch it. Desperate, I rushed to Chair-Lady's house. 'My son is very sick,' I cried to her.

She rushed back with me to the house. And when she saw Noah's condition, she shook her head. 'This is very serious,' she said, with a shake of her head. She had seen a lot of sick people, so she knew what she was talking about.

'Please, help me to save my son,' I begged her.

'Calm down, Ese,' she said, patting me on the shoulder. 'We have to get an herbalist to come and take a look at him. This is not the kind of fever you treat only with neem leave. It is more serious than that.'

'Which herbalist do we consult?' I asked.

'I will go and get one,' she said and left.

★ ★ ★

A little later, she came back with an elderly herbalist. But before then, Pa Umoh and Ma Umoh had turned up. Chair-Lady had informed them that Noah was ill. Ma Umoh was rubbing some ointment on Noah's body when Chair-Lady returned. We gave way for the herbalist to examine Noah, who was drifting in and out of sleep.

Finally, the herbalist straightened up, coughing quietly to clear his throat. His diagnosis made me tremble with fear. 'His condition is very bad,' he said.

'What can be done?' Chair-Lady asked.

'I will do what I can. Let's see how he responds to treatment. If he does not improve in a few days, we may have to get help from afar.'

I began to cry quietly.

'Stop crying, Ese. Crying will do no good,' Ma Umoh said. 'Let's focus on what can be done to get Noah well. He will be well again. Please stop crying.'

'This particular herbalist is very good, I'm sure he will make the boy well,' Chair-Lady said, hopefully.

'I have seen worse fever than this before,' Pa Umoh said. 'The boy will get well again. And you are right, this herbalist is very good.' He nodded at Chair-Lady.

The herbalist had gone into the compound with his bag of herbs to prepare the potions he would administer to Noah. I sat down on the bed, holding Noah's hand. He was covered in sweat; Ma Umoh kept mopping his face and body with a towel. 'You will get well soon,' she whispered to him. And then she moved him gently so she could mop his back.

The herbalist came in moments later. I stood up from the bed to give him space. He had a black potion in a small bowl, and another yellowish potion in a bigger bowl. He carried a cup whose liquid contents I could not see. He arranged the bowls and the cup on a bench. First he made Noah to drink the contents of the cup. Then he rubbed the yellow ointment all over him. And then he rubbed the black ointment on his head and face. I could not recognise my son. He looked like a child wearing a strange makeup. I began to cry quietly.

No one paid any attention to me. The herbalist was now muttering quiet incantations over Noah. He did this for over one hour. Noah drifted off to sleep. I fixed my eyes intently on his face. I could not tell whether he was getting better just by looking at him.

The herbalist gathered his things and took his leave, promising to come back in the evening to examine him. He said Noah was responding well so far. His words drew a murmur of approval.

*   *   *

I felt so grateful for Chair-Lady's support. I had come to realise that she was a good woman, just that she believed so much in tradition. She had prepared some food and made me eat. 'You need strength if you are to look after your son and help him to get well,' she had said.

As news of Noah's illness spread through the village, a steady flow of well-wishers began to come. Some came into the room briefly, others stayed outside, talking in excited voices. They said they were grateful that I took steps to salvage Main Street, even though the rain came and destroyed everything. So they had come to show me support in my darkest hour. They prayed that Noah will get well soon. I thanked them for their support. None of my relatives or in-laws came, and there was no word from the palace.

When Noah woke up in the afternoon, only Chair-Lady and I were in the room, but a few well-wishers were outside. I was seated on the bed while Chair-Lady sat on a stool. Noah opened his eyes slowly and reached for my hand. I leaned over him to study his face.

'Mother,' he called out weakly to me.

'Yes, my son, I'm here. How are you feeling?' I asked.

'Mother, please promise me,' he said.

'I promise you,' I said, even though I did not know what his request was.

'Promise me you'll wake me when I'm gone.'

My entire being began to tremble. I held his face in my hands. 'No, you will not die, my son!' I said, tearfully. 'No, you will not!'

Chair-Lady got up from her stool and stood over us, saying nothing.

'Promise me,' Noah went on. 'Promise you will wake me up.'

'Yes, I will wake you up, my son.'

He gave me a faint smile. Even with the blackness of his face, his smile came through sweetly and it broke my heart.

'Thank you, Mother,' he mumbled. 'My friends, the orphans, please can I see them? And Loko and Luku also.'

I looked up at Chair-Lady In despair.

She gave a soft sigh. 'I will go and get them,' she said and left.

When Chair-Lady returned with the orphans, a hush fell among the well-wishers outside. The boys were shocked to see the way Noah looked. They gathered around his bed anxiously. But in spite of the blackness of his face, his smile was warm and they smiled back warmly at him.

They asked how he was doing, and he told them that he was much better now that he had seen them.

'What did they rub on your face?' Bomboi asked.

'It is medicine to make me well.'

'Oh,' the boy said.

They chatted animatedly for a while. And then Loko and Luku showed up. And when they saw Noah, they began to cry. And the orphans began to cry too.

Chair-Lady and I tried to console them, telling them that Noah would get well soon. But they only cried louder, warranting the people outside to rush inside to see what was amiss. The mood became very sad. His friends would not stop crying, so Noah began to cry too.

I closed my eyes to hold back my tears.

A drizzle began outside, sending everyone scampering to their homes. Only Chair-Lady and the boys remained. We could hear a rumble in the sky. We knew a heavy downpour would come soon.

* * *

By the time the herbalist returned, everyone had sobered up. Noah was sleeping. The rest of us sat quietly in the room. The herbalist was soaked. I gave him a towel to dry himself, and then he examined Noah. He brought out some herbs from his bag and mixed them in a bowl. Then he rubbed the concoction all over Noah's body. We watch intently. Noah continued to sleep. The herbalist began to chant incantations. His voice sounded like that of a spirit being, and it cast a spell of silence on all of us.

After a while, Noah opened his eyes slightly. I rushed to him and took his hand. 'My son,' I called.

'The orphanage,' he said, 'Mother, we must build it for my friends and for the others.'

'Yes, we will build it. Once you get well, we will begin to build it.' In my mind, I swore that I would help him to build the orphanage once he got well.

'And, Mother . . . '

'Yes, my son.'

'Don't forget,' he said.

'No, I won't forget.'

'Wake me when I'm gone.'

'You're not going anywhere,' I whispered fiercely.

'Noah, you cannot go,' Bomboi said tearfully. 'We need you to play with us, please. You're the only friend we have.'

The boys cried silently.

The herbalist shook his head. He turned his face to the wall, muttering quiet but fierce incantations.

That night, the rain poured in torrents, and a mighty wind tore through the village.

★　★　★

After two days of treatment, Noah's condition got no better, and the herbalist said we must get help. 'You have to go and seek the help of a certain herbalist called Mazamaza, who lives in a distant region,' he told me. 'Nobody can undertake the journey for you or with you. You must seek him out yourself, only then could he give you audience and agree to come with you to treat your son. He is a great herbalist, but he doesn't stay in one place, so you must search for him all over. Go and come quickly. While you're away, I will take care of your son. Ask the people you meet on your way, someone may be able to lead you to Mazamaza. As I said, he doesn't stay in one place.'

He suggested that I begin my search for Mazamaza in a certain village which was several hours away, and he gave me directions on how to get there. I carried a jar of water, some bean cake, and money; and I set out before first light. I travelled fast. Soon I left my village behind. As I progressed, I met other pilgrims going to various destinations on one quest or another. Some of them had heard of Mazamaza, but none could tell where to find him.

For a while, we travelled together, and then the roads led us in different directions and I met new pilgrims and we travelled together for a while. When we stopped to eat and rest, we told each other where we were headed and what it was we were seeking. Some said they were in search of wealth, others in search of love. One man said he did not know what he was searching for, but that when he found it he would know. I said I was on a quest to save my son's life. They felt sorry for me; they prayed that I find Mazamaza soon.

I met people who did not speak the same language as me, yet we were able to interact and understand one another. I learnt that language allowed us to say the same things in different tongues, but communication allowed us to relate with one another as human beings. I learnt many things from the people I met and I shared with them the little I knew. And as I travelled from one village to the other in search of Mazamaza, I experienced that gesture of hospitality often extended to strangers in distant lands, which makes a pilgrim's journey to the unknown memorable.

I met people who showed me the way, who gave me shelter and who sustained my hope. I met those who volunteered to travel some way with me, but I told to them that I had to seek out Mazamaza alone as a precondition for him to agree to treat my son. And I met those who told me that I was the most beautiful woman in the world and fell hopelessly in love with me, but I told them that love had to do with the heart and not the looks of a person.

All through these journeys, my mind was preoccupied with thoughts of my son — even when I slept and my tired mind became numb to life itself — and I kept praying that when I got back to my village I would find him alive and well.

And then one afternoon, several days after I had left home, I arrived in a village where a carnival was going on. Everyone was dressed in colourful attires, and those who were not drumming were dancing, and those not dancing were singing. There was assorted food on display by the roadsides for anyone who cared for some. I asked one elderly man if he knew Mazamaza, and he replied that Mazamaza was right there in the village and that the ongoing celebration was in his honour for he had raised someone from the dead.

My heart began to beat uncontrollably and I gripped the man by the hand, forcing him to a halt.

'Please take me to him,' I begged. 'I have travelled for many days and been to many villages in search of him.'

The man studied my face. 'You're a very beautiful woman and you look very tired. I can see that you have travelled for many days,' he said. 'Why do you seek Mazamaza?'

'I seek him to come with me to my village and heal my son. He is sick to the point of death. Take me to Mazamaza, please!'

'It cannot be immediately,' the man said. 'There is a celebration going on.'

'My son is dying. I need to see him straightaway, please.'

And then the man shrugged and told me to follow him.

★ ★ ★

Mazamaza was not a man; he was a young boy of about sixteen. I was very surprised by this discovery.

'I'm looking for a man, an herbalist called Mazamaza,' I said.

'I'm he,' he replied.

For a moment, I was too stunned to speak. 'I have come to see you,' I managed to say. 'I'm from a distant village and I have travelled for many days searching for you.'

'What is it you want of me?'

'My son is sick to the point of death. They said you are the one who can save him from dying.'

He was silent for several moments, his eyes fixed into the distance, as if reading signs in the air. Finally, he focused on me. 'Go back to your village,' he said, 'one day your son will live again.'

'Please come with me and make him well,' I said in a tearful voice.

'I said go back to your village. One day your son will live again. You have come a long way. Hurry back to your village. If you're able to travel fast, you will meet proof that will save you from experiencing a lengthy riddle. Whatever, your son will live again.'

I was confused. 'Please come with me to my village. The herbalist treating my son said I should come back with you.'

'Just go. All will be well.'

'Do as he has said,' the elderly man said to me gently. 'Go, all will be well, as he has said. He is not just an herbalist, he is a spiritualist also. Hurry, go back home.'

The elderly man gave me some food and water. He showed me the road to take, and I set off back to my village.

10

The journey back was quicker. It took me two days. In total, I had been away for ten days. I entered the village as night fell. The noise of people wailing in loud voices came to me, and I wondered why. I was tired and famished, yet I hurried my steps, eager to see my son. The village appeared to be deserted. I took a short cut through Main Street, and as I approached my house, I realised that the entire village had gathered there. The wails became louder when they saw me.

My heart melted inside me. I threw away the jar of water I was carrying, and I ran through the crowd into my house. The living room was packed, I did not notice anyone. I ran into Noah's bedroom. He was not there. I checked my bedroom and then the spare bedroom, but could not find him. I went back into the living room.

'Where is my son?' I asked no one in particular. I got no response, except that the voices of those crying became louder.

I look round. Faces began to register in my mind. I saw Pa Umoh and his wife. I saw Duka, and I saw Chair-Lady among many others. But I did not see the elderly herbalist who had promised to take care of my son.

'Where is my son?' I asked, focusing my eyes on Chair-Lady.

To my surprise, she began to cry. I knew then something had gone wrong. I grabbed her hand. 'Where is my son?' I asked tearfully, but she would not give me an answer.

'Let me explain,' a voice said behind me.

I released Chair-Lady and spun round. To my surprise, I discovered that the Chief had come into the living room, and it was him who had addressed me. 'Let me explain,' he repeated again.

There was quiet in the room now. Only the sound of my harsh breathing could be heard. 'Where is my son?' I repeated, addressing the Chief.

'Let me explain,' he said again.

'Explain what?' I screamed at him.

Everyone began to move away, leaving the Chief and me in the centre of the room. I fixed my eyes upon him, waiting for him to speak. He adjusted the beads around his neck, uncomfortably. He used the horsetail he was holding to fan himself a bit. And then he spoke. 'If only you had arrived an hour earlier you would have seen proof,' he said.

'Seen what proof? Stop talking to me in

riddles and answer my question. Where is my son?'

'He was buried about an hour ago,' he spoke quietly. 'If you had come a little earlier you would have seen him before we buried him. We didn't know you would return today. He died this morning. You know it's our tradition to bury the dead on the same day . . . so I instructed that he should be buried.'

The whole world was spinning wildly around me. All the people in the room began to spin too. I could not hear anything. And soon I could not see anything. A soundless noise started to ring in my ears, and then I fell down with a heavy thud, and all that I had ever known became black.

★ ★ ★

I fell through many worlds, deep, deep, down deep. And I encountered strangeness as I went. I heard loud voices that were silent, and I saw shapes of things that did not exist. I saw a place where people were celebrating, but there was no sound of drums, no singing and no dancing. And I saw that everything was not, and that the world was without form, and void. And when I finally came to a stop, it was night, and I was fast asleep in my bed.

In the morning, I stretched and yawned

and groped on the bed for my son. My eyes were still closed. I could not feel him. I felt certain that he had passed the night in my bed. I opened my eyes and looked. He was not there. I told myself that he must have woken up early and must be somewhere in the house.

'Noah, where are you?' I called out.

Silence greeted me, but I could sense presence in the house. He must be in the backyard, I thought, on the farm, maybe.

I climbed out of bed. And as I walked towards the door, Chair-Lady walked into my bedroom. I was surprised to see her at that time of morning, and in my bedroom for that matter. My face formed into a frown. 'Good morning,' I greeted her. 'Why have you come so early?' I asked.

'You are awake?' She spoke quietly, as if surprised that I was awake.

'I'm just waking up and going in search of my son,' I said. 'Have you seen him? Why have you come so early?'

'Come,' she said, leading me into the living room. I was surprised to see some of my neighbours seated there.

I greeted everyone. 'Is anything the matter?' I asked.

Silence greeted my question and they exchanged puzzled looks amongst themselves.

'Is anything the matter?' I asked again. 'I hope all is well?'

No one responded.

'Ese . . . ' Chair-Lady said, 'you've been out since yesterday.'

'Passed out? How can that be? What happened?' I asked, turning to her.

She sighed. 'Sit down,' she said.

I took my seat, my eyes focused intently on her face. And then everything suddenly came to me.

★ ★ ★

I shot out of my seat, gripped by a great fear. I looked round the room. 'My son! My son! Oh, my son!' I panted. My entire being began to tremble. 'Where is my son?' I screamed. 'Chair-Lady, please where is my son?'

She grabbed me and pushed me back into my seat. Others came to join her to hold me down. 'Relax, Ese, please relax,' Chair-Lady said.

I looked up at her face, begging her with my eyes to tell me the truth.

'She now remembers,' somebody said.

'Noah . . . Noah,' was all I could say as I gasped for breath.

'Noah is dead, and he has been buried,' Chair-Lady said gently.

I knew she was lying. I knew that they had all taken sides with the Chief against me. This was all a lie designed to break me down for refusing to marry the Chief. The Chief must have given them a great amount of money to sell me a lie. I could not believe that Chair-Lady, of all people, would betray me so cruelly. I was racked with agony. So this was the Chief's way of getting back at me — hiding my son somewhere and telling me that he was dead. I raised my voice in a loud cry. Several hands pinned me to my seat. I struggled to break free, but my effort was in vain. I screamed again, pushing this way and that way. Some of the people holding me fell to the ground.

'Chair-Lady, why did you join forces with the Chief to do a wicked thing like this to me? Why would you hide my son and tell me he is dead? Why? Why?' I lamented.

'She does not believe that her son is dead,' someone whispered, the way people whisper when they are trying to hide a wicked lie. And then I knew that, indeed, the Chief had bribed them to tell me that my son was dead.

'My son is not dead. I know he is not dead. Please just take me to him. Take me to him and I will marry the Chief, if that's what you want. Take me to my son, please, I beg you all. I promise I will marry the Chief.' I felt suddenly drained of all energy. I looked up silently at the faces of the people holding me down. And I was surprised to see that Duka and Pa Umoh and his wife were among them. And then I saw my parents and Tanto's parents, and I knew that, indeed, the whole village had sold out. 'How much did the Chief pay you to do this to me?' I asked, directing my question to my parents and in-laws. 'Tell me, how much did he pay you?' I shook my head hopelessly.

'She does not believe,' another person said, as if warning the rest of them that their lie was not working.

Of course, their lie was not working. I knew that the Chief was behind this cruel plot, and I knew it was because I refused to marry him. I shook my head slowly; I could not find words to express my disappointment at their behaviour.

'Maybe if we take her to her son's grave she would believe,' someone said.

'I think that's the best thing to do,' another said.

'Okay, let's take her there,' Chair-Lady said.

'I'm not going anywhere,' I protested.

They lifted me up on my feet.

'I said I'm not going anywhere!' I repeated. 'Enough of your wicked lies! My son is not in a grave, you have hidden him somewhere, and you must bring him out.'

They tried to get me to walk out of the living room, but I resisted with all my strength. They tried and tried, but I would not move. Finally they lifted me on their heads, took me out of the room, and headed to the graveyard. I struggled and screamed at the top of my voice, demanding that they put me down. None of them said a word until we got to the graveyard. Finally, they set me down. 'That's your son's grave,' Chair-Lady said, pointing to a fresh mound of earth.

My sorrow turned into anger. I stopped crying, and I shouted at them, 'My son is not in there.'

'He is in there,' Chair-Lady said. 'He was buried there yesterday.'

'Then dig him out let's see,' I challenged her.

They all gasped.

'Ese, you know it is an abomination to dig up the dead,' Chair-Lady said.

'Yes, it is an abomination. But my son is not dead, and he is not in that grave. So dig it up let's see. This is all a part of your wicked lie.'

They spoke and argued amongst themselves for a few moments. And then they carried me back to my house the same way they had brought me.

* * *

When we got to my house, I saw the orphans standing at a distance, their arms across their chests. I called out to them, but I was rushed into the house and not allowed to talk to them.

They took me into my room and laid me on the bed. I had become too weak and too sad to fight. So I closed my eyes and drifted into sleep.

It was starting to get dark when I awoke. Everyone had gone, only Chair-Lady remained. She told me she had moved in with me to look after me for a while. I said nothing in response. I simply stared at her. We stayed in silence. I wondered where they were hiding Noah — probably in the palace. I told myself that I must find a way to get in there and rescue him.

Chair-Lady went to the kitchen and brought me food. She begged me to eat. I ate and drank a little, then I pushed the plates away. I stared at her, waiting for her to tell me the truth, to beg me and tell me she did it for money, and that she would help me to get my son back from the palace. But she said nothing, and I knew that her heart was set.

As for my parents and in-laws, I could not believe they had turned into such monsters to betray me as cruelly as they had done. I shook my head.

*   *   *

A few days passed. Chair-Lady slept in the house with me at night, on a mat in the living room. In the morning she made breakfast for me before going to her house. She came and went during the day. I noticed a couple of guards outside my house, probably assigned there to watch me and prevent me from taking any steps that could expose the lie about my son. I knew I could not fight the Chief and the entire village, so I told myself to tread carefully. At the right time their lie would be exposed and I would be reunited with my son again.

I spent my time sleeping or just sitting in the backyard gazing at nothing. I could not think of anything. Sometimes the rain fell without ceasing, and the wind was louder and angrier than before. I did not know what was happening in the village because I had not stepped a foot outside my house since they brought me back from the graveyard. I knew I must go to the palace soon to confront the

Chief. And I reminded myself to visit the orphans to tell them what was going on.

On the fifth morning, I had gathered enough strength. After I had taken a bath and eaten, I told Chair-Lady that I was going to the palace.

'To go and do what?' she asked.

'To see the Chief and tell him to give me my son,' I said resolutely.

'Your son is not at the palace,' Chair-Lady said, quietly.

I saw fear in her eyes — fear that their lie would be exposed very soon.

I confronted her boldly. 'That's what you say, but I can see it in your eyes that you're lying. Why, Chair-Lady? Why did you betray me so cruelly?'

She sighed and looked away, saying nothing. Of course, she had nothing to say. She knew that I was saying the truth.

'I didn't betray you,' she said, 'and it is pointless going to the palace.'

'Well, I'm going, and there is nothing you or anyone can do to stop me. After all, I'm not under arrest.'

'Ese, take it easy. With time everything will become very clear to you.'

I did not answer her. I stormed out of the house. The guards outside did not try to stop me. As I went through the village, the people

I met greeted me, commiserating with me over my son's death. I did not answer them. I knew they were only trying to keep up the lie.

When I got to the palace, the royal guards shook their heads sadly at me, expressing their condolences in quiet voices. I shook my head with a bitter laugh. I know all your lies, I thought to myself. Aloud, I said to them, 'I would like to see the Chief.'

They exchanged worried looks, unsure what to do. Getting no response from them, I marched into the palace. They scrambled after me, but none of them tried to stop me. I entered a large hall. Colourful mats were spread out on the floor to serve as seats, and the heads of various wild animals were mounted all over the wall. The hall was empty, so I proceeded into the next room, which was much smaller. In this room, more mats were spread out on the floor, but the wall was bare. There was a big drum in each corner of the room. Beside each drum was a large bowl containing ashes. Two guards carrying swords were positioned at the far door that led deeper into the palace. As I approached the door, the guards lifted their sword. 'You cannot go beyond this point,' one of them said.

'I want to see the Chief,' I said stubbornly. But they merely stared at me, saying nothing.

'I said I want to see the chief,' I shouted at the top of my voice.

And then the Chief came out and walked towards me with some anxiety.

'Give me back my son,' I snapped at him.

'Your son . . . ,' he said, looking at me in confusion.

'Don't give me that look. You have him here in the palace. I want my son back.'

'Your son is not here,' he said. 'Your son is dead.'

'No, my son is not dead. Please just give him back to me and I will marry you, if that's what you want.'

The Chief began to tremble. 'Please marry me,' he said. 'When I had the painting, I let you be because I had you, even if only in a painting. But then those useless thieves came and stole you from me.' He stretched his hands towards me. 'Ese, please marry me.'

The guards and I gave gasps of surprise. It was the Chief who had stolen the painting; he had admitted to it in the presence of his guards. Unfortunately, he was the Chief, so there was nothing anyone could do. But we now knew that the Chief was the thief. His guards were not supposed to divulge his confession to the public, but I knew that they would gossip about it all the same.

I could not be bothered about the painting.

All I wanted was my son. 'Give me my son and I will marry you,' I said.

And then he broke down in tears. The guards looked on in confusion, not knowing how to handle the situation.

'I swear your son is not here,' the Chief said.

'Then let me check the entire palace and see for myself.'

'Go ahead,' he said to me. To the guards, he said, 'Take her round. Let her search the whole palace and see for herself.'

I searched the whole palace, but there was no sign of Noah. I had never felt so much frustration. I could not fathom where they could have hidden my son.

★ ★ ★

Not knowing what to do, I left the palace and made my way slowly to the outskirts. I found the orphans at home. They were lying on the floor in the living room, looking lost, silent tears in their eyes. They stared at me with pity, unable to say a word.

I sat down on the floor with them, my back against the wall. 'They've taken Noah away,' I told them. 'I don't know where they've taken him.'

I got no response.

After a while, I got up and went round to wipe their tears. I noticed that they looked gaunt, as if they had not eaten in days. I got a tuber of yam from their barn and cooked it. I fried pepper and tomatoes in red oil. I set the table and told them to come and eat, but they just stared at me. I pleaded with them to eat, promising to take them to my house to live with me. They looked at me uncertainly, hopefully. And then Mofe rose and told the others to stand up. They obeyed him, and they ate.

I watched them eat. None of us said a word. When they finished, I did the dishes and joined them on the floor of the living room. Suddenly, the thunder rumbled in the distance. I got up and looked outside. I saw that the rain would begin soon. I turned to them and said, 'Get some of your things, we're going to my house.'

They scrambled to their feet and got a few things. We hurried back to the village before the rain could start.

★ ★ ★

Chair-Lady was shocked when I arrived with them.

I told Bomboi and Igalo to put up in Noah's room while Mofe and Tega took up the spare room. I made up my mind to convert the entire house into an orphanage. The rooms were very large; I could partition them to get three extra rooms. I planned to commence the project the next day. When Noah eventually returned home, he would be proud to see what I had done.

'Why did you bring the boys?' Chair-Lady asked, looking agitated.

'I brought them to live with me, and I intend to convert my house into an orphanage,' I told her. 'I will carve out extra rooms, and I will make the whole house colourful and bright, just the way Noah saw it in his dream. In time, I will build more rooms in the backyard and take in more children like these.'

Chair-Lady was speechless. She hurried out. She did not come to sleep in the house that night or the nights that followed.

* * *

While I helped them to unpack their things, Bomboi sat quietly on a stool, his hands in his lap, his eyes following my movements. The older boys helped me with this and that.

The rain had started to fall. The wind was loud, and the village appeared to be empty. In fact, the whole world was empty;

157

we were all on our own.

We finished unpacking and went into the living room. I left the lantern in a corner. Bomboi sat beside me on a small bench, the others sat on a longer one. We sat in silence, but we could read each other's mind — we were each thinking of Noah, and missing him. We were sad. We were not complete without him.

Finally, Bomboi asked, 'Mother, where is Noah?'

I was surprised and delighted that he called me Mother. I placed my arm around him. 'Noah will come home soon,' I said to him. 'I will find him and bring him home soon.'

'But they said Noah is dead,' he said and began to cry.

I pulled him to me. 'Stop crying, please,' I told him. 'Noah is not dead. It's all a lie made up by the Chief. Noah will return home soon.'

'We saw the grave,' Mofe said. 'We saw them carry the . . . '

I cut him off. 'It's all a part of their wicked lie. Noah is not dead. They're keeping him somewhere. I don't know where, but I will find him soon and bring him home. And all of us will live together happily ever after. You will see.'

Mofe shook his head sadly, saying nothing. That night, I listened to strange enchantments in the night while the boys slept.

11

For three days, no one came near us, but the entire village was buzzing with the news that the orphans had moved in with me.

We had started making the blocks which we would use to partition the rooms. Mofe, Tega and I did most of the work while Igalo and Bomboi helped with the little bits. When it was not raining, we dug mud from the backyard and deposited it in a heap in the living room. We could not make the blocks outside because they could be destroyed by rain, so we used the living room, having moved the furniture and other items into my room. We arranged the blocks in columns, leaving enough space between them for movement.

While we dug mud in the backyard, several people gathered to watch us from afar. We did not bother about them, but we could hear their excited voices as they talked about us, asking each other what we were doing. They were mostly women and children; their curiosity drew a few men, who watched us for a while then left to spread the word about what they had seen.

I undertook the work readily. But sometimes I could not help being weighed down by thoughts of my son. At such times, I reminded myself that I was preparing our home for his joyous return, and this lifted my spirit again. I felt really grateful to have the boys living with me — they all called me Mother now, and I referred to them as my sons. We had become family; I could not wait for Noah to join us. I made up my mind to go back to the palace in a few days' time to demand his release. Surely, the Chief could not keep him forever. I imagined the delight on his face when he returned and discovered that I had converted our house into an orphanage and that his friends now lived with us. I felt thrilled and I worked harder than ever before.

★　★　★

When it was time for me to cook, we took a break and went to the kitchen together. I figured that the food in the barn would last us about a month. Then I would have to travel to other markets to buy food. But that was not a problem; I had saved some money while business was good on Main Street.

We chatted animatedly about our progress while I cooked. After we had eaten, we rested for a while before going back to work. By the end of the third day we had made about twenty blocks, and I estimated that we would need about two hundred for the work that I had in mind.

Our world crumbled on the afternoon of the fourth day when the Chief, the priests and a small crowd showed up at our house. The crowd waited outside while the Chief and the priests came into the living room. They were shocked to see the work we were doing, and for a while they just gaped at us. They moved gingerly between the columns of blocks, like wary inspectors assessing a poorly done job, and they shook their heads in disbelief.

'What are you doing?' the High Priest asked in astonishment.

'We are making blocks to build more rooms,' I replied nonchalantly.

'Are you aware that it's against the law for women to build in our village? Are you aware it's the worst taboo you can think of? And that any woman who breaks the law faces death by hanging? Are you aware?' the High Priest asked.

I turned to the Chief. 'So it's not enough that you have kidnapped my son, you have now come to intimidate me with the priests. Is that it?' I asked angrily.

The Chief shook his head hopelessly. 'I told them to leave you alone,' he said, in a resigned voice, 'but they wouldn't listen to me. They dragged me here because I'm the custodian of our laws, and they said I must act or they would take me to the shrine and invoke the wrath of the gods upon me and drive me mad. I had to come with them. Ese, please forgive me and marry me,' he wailed pathetically.

'Enough!' I snapped, raising my hand. I turned to the priests. 'Go and tell the gods, there is nothing anyone can do to stop me. These boys are my children now. They call me Mother and I call them my sons. They will live here in my house.'

Chair-Lady barged in then. A gasp of horror escaped her when she saw the mud and the blocks we had made. 'Ese, you're playing with fire,' she wailed, as if her entire being had been torched. 'What do you think you are doing?'

'What do you see me doing?' I retorted.

She placed her hands on her head in frustration.

'You have committed a grave offence, and you will face the law duly,' the High Priest said to me, his voice like a whip.

'I have committed no offence,' I replied fearlessly.

'You have committed no offence, you say?'

'I have committed no offence!'

'We shall see!' He turned to the Chief and his fellow priests. 'Let's go.'

The Chief tried to say something, but the High Priest grabbed his arm and led him away. Chair-Lady followed them, screaming as if a terrible disaster had befallen her.

The boys looked very frightened. I told them not to worry, that everything would be fine. I was cold with fear inside, but I refused to let the boys notice it.

★ ★ ★

It was dark when Loko came. He said he had sneaked away from home to bring me vital information. He was cold with fear. 'They're going to execute you by hanging tomorrow,' he told me and began to cry.

The boys began to cry too, and I tried to no avail to quieten them. 'God in heaven will not let it happen,' I told them. 'Please stop crying.'

'The news is all over the village,' Loko continued. 'You must leave tonight. If you don't, they will hang you tomorrow. I had to come to tell you. If my father knows he will kill me. Please leave tonight.'

'I cannot leave,' I said. 'I cannot leave my

children behind. And I need to find Noah. I need to find him.' My voice was raw with grief.

Suddenly, the door creaked open, startling us. It was Chair-Lady. I was surprised; I did not expect her to come back. 'Ah, Ese!' she lamented, shaking her head. 'Ah, Ese, I'm forced to agree that you're a good and strong woman. But you cannot fight tradition. It was given to us by the gods, and you cannot fight the gods. You must leave tonight or else you will die by hanging tomorrow. The priests have taken a decision, no one can save you. Leave, please.'

'I'm going nowhere,' I snapped.

Again she shook her head. 'Come with me, let me show you something,' she said. 'Let me show you something, and then you can make up your mind.'

'I'm going nowhere with you, except you want to show me my son.'

'I cannot show you your son, but I can show you something that will help you to make up your mind. Come with me, please. After you have seen it, I will never bother you again. I promise. I will leave you to do whatever you want. You will never see me in your house again. You will never hear your name on my lips again.' She went on her knees. 'Come with me, please,' she begged.

In spite of myself, I decided to go with her and see what she had to show me. The boys and I followed her, and she hurriedly led us to the centre of Main Street, where she pointed to a giant tree with the torchlight she was holding. Dangling high up from the tree was a thick noose. 'That's the rope they will use to hang you tomorrow,' she said. 'I have come to warn you because I don't want my last memory of you to be your body dangling from a tree. Please leave tonight. I will make sure that you're not stopped by the guards or anyone. I will do it as my parting gift to you.' She turned abruptly and left us at the foot of the tree.

★ ★ ★

Loko led the way as we headed back home. I held Bomboi by the hand. We walked quickly, quietly, as if there was an urgent rhythm in the night. My heart was heavy with sorrow. I wondered what would happen to Noah and the rest of my children if I was hung. But I could not take the decision to leave them behind. No, I could not. Somehow, I had hope that something would happen to swing things in my favour. For the first time in a while, I thought of Kpofe. And I prayed that he would come from the city, like the last time. He had told me that all we could do was hope and pray. So I hoped and prayed that he would come.

When we got home, Loko took both of my hands. 'Please you must leave or else they will kill you tomorrow,' he said. 'Leave!' Tears were streaming down his face.

I began to cry too, 'I cannot leave my children behind,' I lamented.

'If you leave, you will see them again one day, but if you don't, you never will,' Loko said. 'Go, please.'

I shook my head. They were seated with me on my bed. Bomboi had his head on my lap. He was terribly exhausted. I could feel his heartbeat hard and fast. I rubbed his back gently, to calm his breathing. 'I must find Noah. I must look after my children,' I said fiercely, as if speaking to myself.

'Don't worry about Noah and the rest of your children. They will be okay,' Loko said.

'Mother, do as he has said,' Mofe said. 'Go for our sake. We will see again one day. You will see Noah too. But if you stay you will die, and we will never see you again. Please do as Loko has said. Please go for our sake.'

Tega and Igalo begged me to go too. Only Bomboi did not say a word. He had started dozing. Now and then, he would raise his head, look at me and place his head back on my lap. Although he did not say anything, I could see the silent plea in his eyes. I could tell that he too was begging me to leave. And as I rubbed his back, he suddenly began to cry very loudly. My heart became too sad. I placed him on the bed. After a while he stopped crying, and I realised that he had fallen asleep. I covered him with a blanket. Soon, Igalo fell asleep too.

For a brief moment there was total quiet. I knew then that I had to go. I got up and packed a few things. I brought out a pouch containing all the money that I had. I gave some to Mofe. 'Use this for your brothers and yourself,' I told him. 'Stay here in the house, don't go back to the outskirts. Be strong. When Noah is released, he will stay with you. I will come back for all of you one day. Loko and Luku will be your friends, they will help you.'

I wiped my tears and smiled round at them. I bent down to kiss Bomboi and Igalo on the cheek — they were fast asleep, breathing as if they had fear in their stomach.

I told myself that I would be strong, that I would not cry anymore, until the day I saw all my children again. Loko, Mofe and Tega surrounded me in a hug, and then they led me into the dark night.

We headed briskly out of the village,

avoiding Main Street. And as we went, we passed guards who looked the other way, allowing me a smooth passage. The boys escorted me up to the abandoned building in the outskirts. And then we exchanged goodbyes. None of us cried. We just hugged, silently, as if words would destroy all that we wanted to preserve.

12

I journeyed with a heavy heart, sleeping wherever I could lay my head. Along the way, I met bandits who, instead of robbing me, gave me money and provision after they had listened to my sad story. I met nomads who provided me with food and water. And I met a seer who prayed for me and assured me that no harm would come to me.

I arrived in a small village a month's journey by foot from the village of my birth. It was at the gate of the village that I met Mama, the kindly old widow who took me in. I told her about myself. She felt sad that I was a widow at such a young age. But she said she was very happy that I had come. After I had taken a bath and eaten, she told me about herself. She said she would die soon, that she had only been waiting for me to come. My heart raced and I asked her what she meant. She sighed and told me to pull my seat closer.

'Long before now,' she began, 'a prophet predicted your coming. He said you would come from a distant village, a beautiful young widow, with two gold earrings.' She paused, studied me and asked, 'Do you have two gold earrings?' I shook my head. 'Well, never mind . . . ,' she continued. 'He said when you arrived I should know that my time to go had come. You see, twenty years ago when I lost my husband and three children, I had wanted to take my own life. They were fishermen. They caught a strange sickness from the river, and they died one after the other in a matter of days. I was fifty years old then. My world caved in, and I prepared a poisonous potion which I intended to drink so I could die and join them in the other world. As I was about to take the potion, the prophet walked into this very room and told me to stop. He said my time had not come, and he told me about your coming.

'He said we would meet at the gate of the village; that you will be tired and famished having travelled a great distance. He warned me that I must not allow you to continue to another village. He said if I did, we would spend many painful years trying to find each other again. And he told me that I must take you as my daughter.' She smiled brightly at me.

I was speechless.

'Don't be sad about the children you left behind,' she continued, looking deep into my eyes. 'This is your home now.' She spread her hands to indicate the mighty house comprising over twelve rooms. 'And this is your destiny. The whole village knows that you are coming; I have told them about you. Do not be sad. Instead, be strong and happy, and only then can you fulfil your destiny.

'Remember, I lost my husband and my children, yet I waited for you for twenty years. I was sad at first, but afterwards, I lived every day with happiness and a sense of purpose. Now I have fulfilled my destiny. You must learn to be strong and happy if you are to fulfil yours.' And then she warned me, 'Never tell anyone else the reason why you fled your village. Your village and ours have similar traditions. If they know, they will not accept you here.'

★ ★ ★

Three days later, Mama passed away peacefully in her sleep, and the entire village gathered to mourn her. After the burial, sympathisers came to visit me in droves. They had all heard about me. And they asked why it took me so long to come. They referred to me as Mama's daughter; they prayed that I find the fortitude to bear my loss. I could not help being amazed; I had been in the village for just a few days, yet everyone knew me.

Surely, destiny was leading me; but I felt alone and deeply saddened by Mama's death.

The Chief of the village came to visit me too. He was a handsome young man who had recently taken over the throne from his late father. I felt greatly troubled when he arrived on a white horse. A rush of bad memories came to me. He noticed my agitation; he smiled and told me that he had come in peace.

'Mama was a great woman,' he said, when he had taken a seat. 'She told us about you long before you arrived. She said she was waiting for you to come and then she would go. We never really believed her. But it happened exactly as she had said, and we are all amazed.'

I did not know what to say. I averted my eyes.

'What's your name?' he asked.

'My name is Ese,' I replied.

'It's a nice name. I have never heard a name like that,' he said, with a nod of his head. 'If there is anything you need, please come to the palace to see me and I will do my best to help.' He rose to leave.

I thought he looked clumsy in his regalia. Somehow, I sensed that he was not cut out to be a chief. I quickly pushed this thought away from my mind, and I thanked him for coming. Long after he had galloped away on his horse, I was overcome by painful memories. I wondered what was happening to my children, Noah especially. My heart became terribly sad. But I remembered what Mama had said, about being strong and happy if I was to fulfil my destiny.

★ ★ ★

I drew inspiration from Mama's story. I could hear her voice talking to me. In a way, our stories were similar. Certainly, our destinies were connected.

It seemed like ages since I had arrived in that village, but it had been less than a week, and so much had happened in that time. For the first time, I went for a walk on a quiet evening. I remembered one or two faces who had paid me condolence visits. I made an effort to memorise as many names and faces as possible as I went. They did not greet me as though I was a stranger, but as if they had known me all their lives, and this made me feel so much at home. The children were warm and lively; I greeted them with affection, trying not to allow memories overcome me.

I noted that the houses were built of mud, that they all had tall thatched roofs. And I could tell that it was a prosperous village for I saw people returning from the farms bearing fresh produce. I wondered what their market looked like, whether it was anything like Main Street. I told myself to visit the market soon.

A young man carrying a small cellophane bag containing assorted fruits approached me. He greeted me with a smile, and I returned his greeting. Other young men gathered at a distance to watch enviously. 'I was going to bring this to you at home,' he said, opening the bag for me to see. 'I was at the burial and I saw you.' He hesitated. 'I'm sorry about Mama's death.'

'Oh, thank you,' I said. 'It was kind of you to have come for Mama's burial.'

'I will follow you home and drop this off.' He raised the bag.

'I very much appreciate your kind gesture . . . ' I hesitated and smiled, not wanting to hurt his feelings. 'I mean, you don't have to give those to me.'

'I want you to have them, please,' he said. 'I got them from the farm for you. It's good to be nice to strangers. Not that you're a stranger amongst us, still . . . '

'Okay, thanks,' I said. 'I was just taking a walk to get to know the village a little.'

We walked on together.

'Do you like our village?' he asked.

'It's beautiful and I think the people are very kind.'

'Why did it take you so long to come?' he asked. 'Mama waited for you for a long time. She told us she was waiting for you. She said that you are a very beautiful widow, but we didn't believe her then. And now you have come. But you don't look like a widow to me. You are too young to be a widow.'

We passed a group of children playing football on a small field. Memories threatened to overwhelm me. Mama's voice whispered a reminder in my ear. I smiled and waved at the children.

'I'm a widow,' I said with a shrug, turning to the young man.

'It's strange,' he said, as if his mind was in a distant place.

'Well . . . I'm a widow,' I repeated.

'My name is Kewe,' he told me.

'It's a pleasure meeting you,' I said. 'I'm Ese.'

'I know. We all know your name. No one bears that name in the whole of this village.'

'That's what the Chief said. The palace, I would like to see what the palace looks like,' I said to him.

'Let's go this way, I will show you,' Kewe said.

The palace was a mighty compound

comprising several mud houses with towering roofs. It was fenced round by a large wall, and it had a giant wooden gate. It looked majestic indeed, far bigger than the palace in my village. As we walked by, I saw a few guards who waved friendly at us. They did not carry sticks or swords; they just walked around with their hands in their pockets. I was amazed by this and I wondered how they would defend the palace in the event of an attack.

'The guards don't have sticks or swords,' I said to Kewe. 'With what would they defend the palace?'

'They don't need to carry sticks or swords,' he explained. 'This is a peaceful village. We've never had any violence. But if the village or the palace ever came under attack, there is an arsenal of weapons and charms in the palace they could use.' He gave a deep chuckle.

'It's good that your village is peaceful,' I said. 'And your chief, he is such a young man. I thought he would be old.'

'He took over the throne from his father, who died not too long ago. You see, he had left the village for the city some years ago. But when his father died, he had to come back. The oracle said he was the chosen one. He has older brothers who live here in the village, yet the oracle chose him. At first he did not want to come, but he began to suffer one

177

misfortune after the other in the city. The High Priest sent message to him that unless he comes to take over the throne he would continue to experience bad luck. So he had to come to take over the throne, and he married his childhood love whom he had left behind in the village. They said he could marry as many wives as he liked, but he said he was okay with one. He is a good chief. He is doing things differently.'

'It's all so interesting. I had better return home though, to relieve you of that burden,' I said, pointing to the bag in his hand.

'I could carry it forever,' he said, and we both laughed.

The sun had dipped. Smoke was rising from every kitchen, and delicious aromas suffused the evening air. We got to my house and he handed the bag to me at the gate. I thanked him once again, and we exchanged goodbyes.

★   ★   ★

The house Mama left me had thirteen rooms and a sprawling living room. Apart from the palace, it was the biggest house in the village. Before she died she told me the history of the house. It was built by her husband, who was one of the wealthiest people in the region.

They had planned to have many children. But after they had three sons, she could no longer conceive.

Their children grew up and, following in the footsteps of their father, they became fishermen. Fishmongers came from far and near to buy from them at the rivers where they caught fish, and their family gradually amassed a fortune. Her husband planned to build three more mansions, one for each son. And just when he was preparing to lay the foundation of the first, death knocked cruelly on their door. The villagers had wanted to brand Mama a witch and condemn her to death, but the prophet who predicted my coming came to her rescue and forbade anyone to trouble her, saying that she was a good woman. He was a renowned prophet, so they believed him.

Mama had wanted to sell the house and move to a smaller one, but the prophet told her not to. He told her that the house would be put to its rightful use at the appointed time. So she lived in the house with her nieces and nephews and cousins and various relatives. But as they grew older and got married, they left one after the other, until only Mama remained.

She hired maids who came daily to tend the house and the garden in the backyard.

When the house became too empty for her to live in alone, she got the helps to stay nights in shifts. She was a rich woman; her husband had left her a fortune, so she lived in relative comfort and ensured that the house was well-kept.

I inherited Mama's wealth and I carried on with her policy of using maids who stayed nights in the house in shifts. They told me the small histories of the house which Mama had been unable to tell me. And, gradually, the picture of a charming and loving family that had lived there a long time ago formed in my mind.

★   ★   ★

And they told me about their customs and tradition, and I became greatly dismayed to learn that orphans were also regarded as evil children and treated as slaves in that village. They said Mama had tried to convert her house into an orphanage, but the chief at that time, the father of the current chief, and most of his subjects resisted the idea fiercely for they were a people who believed very much in tradition.

Once again, I had found myself in a village where tradition could pit me against the people and the authorities. I thought of leaving. But I remembered that Mama had told me that this was my destiny. She had also told me to be strong and happy. I wondered how it was possible to be strong and happy in a place where orphans were treated very poorly. And it occurred to me that being weak and sad would not change anything.

Soluso told me about the orphans. He was a young man who spoke in a quiet voice and helped me with chores around the house. He told me that there were not many orphans in the village, so a stranger could not so easily tell of their existence. 'But they are quite easy to identify when you come across them,' he said. 'They look very malnourished and sad; and, often, they scavenge for food.'

'I have taken a walk around the village,' I said to him, 'but I haven't seen any child that looked malnourished and sad, or one scavenging for food.'

'That's because there are few of them, and they are always working out of sight in compounds or on remote farms,' he said. 'You rarely come across them in the street. When they go to search the rubbish heaps for food, they avoid making contact with people. And they take to their heels when they see anyone approaching.'

'But it's not their fault that they lost their parents,' I said in despair.

'Mama was of the same position. And she always told us that one day this house would become a place of refuge for orphans.'

I nodded silently at Soluso's words. Somehow, I sensed that destiny was speaking to me through him. Afterwards, as I sat alone and gazed into space, I started to understand what destiny was saying to me — that I had been chosen for a mission.

* * *

I paid the Chief a visit. He was very glad to see me and he welcomed me warmly. It surprised me that his wife attended to me herself even though there were several servants in the palace. She was a beautiful and nice woman. She brought me water and some fruits, and then she retreated and left the Chief and me alone.

'How are you finding our village so far?' the Chief asked

'Your majesty, I thought it was lovely, until I learnt that orphans are not treated well here,' I replied frankly but politely.

His jaws hardened, and for a moment he was silent. He asked, 'Have you seen any?'

'No, I haven't, but I have heard about them, that they're branded to be evil children and treated as slaves.'

We fell into silence. I could not say whether he was angry, so I kept quiet and waited for him to speak. Finally, he sighed and sat forward. 'My father sat on this throne for ages,' he said. 'After he died the oracle picked me to succeed him. I didn't want to, but in the end I had no choice. When I climbed the throne, I realised that there are many changes I would love to see, but I also realised that I could not promote those changes all by myself. I'm only the custodian of our traditions, and there's very little I can do to change things.

'You see, for change to happen, the people must be willing to conform to it, they must be prepared to drive it. But in the short time that I have been on this throne, I have come to realise that the people are averse to change. And I have also come to realise that, ultimately, power belongs to the people.

'I'm not sure if you are aware that before she died Mama had tried to take some orphans into her care, but my father, the chief at the time, and the people vehemently opposed her, and she had to give up. Of course, the people and the Chief are controlled by the priests. But where the people truly want change and they get the backing of the Chief, the priests become powerless. What I'm trying to say, in essence, is that I want to see many changes in this village, but I need the people to work with me for that to happen.'

He leaned forward a bit more, hardening his jaws. 'I will conspire with you,' he said in a quiet voice. 'Promote the changes you want to see, and you will get my support, and together we can ensure that orphans get the good care they deserve. I do not need to tell you more.' He sighed and sat back.

★   ★   ★

I returned home happy. I had nothing to be sad about anymore. All my sadness had been eased. And now I must pursue that destiny that could only be realised through strength and happiness.

I summoned Soluso. He came eagerly. 'Looks like it's going to rain today,' he said and smiled. 'We haven't had rain for a while.'

'I hope it rains,' I said.

'Is there anything I can do for you?' he asked.

'Yes, but take a seat first.'

He sat down, his eyes focused on my face.

'Tell me about the priests of this village,' I said.

'They're very powerful,' he said.

'Apart from that?'

He hesitated, thinking. 'They make laws and get the Chief to assent to them. They claim that every law they make is given to them by the gods. And everybody must follow the laws to the letter.'

'What if the people and the Chief reject their laws? What can they do?'

'The Chief and the people together, nothing. The Chief alone cannot reject their laws, and the people alone cannot reject them either. The consequence of rejecting or disobeying their laws is so terrible no one dares to do so.'

'And what's the consequence?'

'They say that the consequence of rejecting or disobeying the laws of the gods is blindness, and then madness and then death. No one wants to go blind and run mad before dying. We are all afraid, so we accept the laws they make.'

'But do you believe what they say? Has anyone died in the manner that they describe?'

'Not believing is in itself a crime. You can't come out and say that you do not believe. We all believe. And because we believe, no one has ever died as they describe,' he said with a shrug.

'Thank you for sharing your knowledge with me,' I said to him.

He rose to leave. 'Let me know if you need more information,' he said.

I smiled at him.

As the rain poured that night, I sat alone by the lantern and thought of many things. I thought of my children. I thought of Kpofe faraway in the big city. And I thought of the stolen painting which the late High Priest said would be the key to a great destiny. For a moment, I wondered how that would come about. And then I told myself that it was not for me to worry about how destiny would fulfil itself.

I slept soundly, and I did not feel any sadness inside me, only resolve to follow destiny with happiness.

★ ★ ★

The following day was market-day. I went to see what the market looked like, and I was surprised to discover that it was similar to Main Street, only that it was located in a square and was simply known as 'market'. There were several wooden stalls of different shapes and sizes scattered all over the market, and the air was thick with dust. It was easy to identify the merchants who came from afar. They wore colourful half-coats and small caps embroidered with exotic designs. And they chatted loudly with everyone, smiling broadly to show that business was good.

It was a big market. On a few occasions, I lost Oyi, a young woman who had been working as a maid in Mama's house and had accompanied me to the market in order to help me carry my shopping. The dust was so much you are sometimes unable to see the faces of people clearly. For a moment I wondered what had become of Main Street. I wondered also, if I would come across some of the merchants I used to supply with vegetables. I was excited by the prospect. And I walked all over the market, again and again, until my legs became weary. Sadly, I did not come across any of the merchants I used to know. I thought of Chair-Lady and I wondered if she had managed to revive Main Street.

I bought a few things, which Oyi carried in a basket. She explained that the market took place weekly, and she advised me get whatever I would need for the next week.

Oyi was about five years younger than me and had only been married for a few months. She had been working for Mama for many years, and she was very happy to transfer her service to me. I liked her. She always wore a smile, and she was shy but unpretentious. When she wasn't working for me, she practised sewing on a Singer machine that Mama had bought for her. She said her ambition was to become a tailor, and she hoped to take her designs to the big city one day.

I told her about Kpofe and his girlfriend who worked in a garment factory in the city. I told her that if she ever went to the city with her designs, she should ask for a young man called Kpofe, who would introduce her to Eliza, who could help her break into the garment industry. She was very excited and she told me she would work harder to accomplish her dream knowing this. Of course, I had no idea how big the city was or how either of us could ever find Kpofe there.

When we were done at the market, I told her to take our shopping home while I went for a stroll to the gate of the village.

'It's simply called The Gate,' she said with a grin.

'Hmm, it sounds romantic,' I said.

'Young couples on dates often hang out there,' she told me. 'My husband used to take me there, before we got married. Not anymore. I'm an old woman now.' She laughed.

'We all become old women once we get married.' I laughed too.

'You don't want me to come with you?' she asked.

'I will be okay,' I said to her with a smile. 'I will see you in a bit.

* * *

It was nothing like a gate. The Gate was the point where the road leading into the village broadened and then narrowed and houses began to dot the landscape to the left and to the right. That point where the road broadened was actually the part referred to as The Gate. Several small rocks, which were used as seats, could be found there, and I sat on the very rock on which I had found Mama sitting on the day I arrived in the village.

In the distance, I saw a boy and a girl walking hand in hand. I smiled to myself, thinking that they would probably stop taking such romantic walks once they became married.

I touched the rock as memories of Mama came to me. Destiny was such a funny thing, I said to myself. I sat there alone in the sun admiring the beautiful landscapes that spread into the forest in the distance. I wondered what the forest looked like, whether there were wild animals inside it, or just trees and tall grasses and spirits. I recollected that Mama had risen from the rock when she saw me approaching. And when I reached her, she had smiled at me and said, 'You must have been travelling for a long time.'

It was obvious — I looked dirty and tired and I was famished for I hadn't eaten anything that day.

'Yes,' I replied weakly. 'I'm a widow and I have been travelling for about a month.'

I noticed a slight change in her expression — as if she was both surprised and shocked at the same time. 'Come, take a seat,' she said, leading me to the rock on which she had been sitting. 'You look very tired.' There was concern in her voice.

After I had rested a bit, she helped me up and took me to her house.

I smiled at the memories.

In the distance, I could still see the lovers. I stood up to go back to the village. For a moment, I looked round The Gate, and I told myself that I would repeat the visit the following day at about the time that I had found Mama there.

13

I returned to The Gate the following evening. It was deserted, and I took my seat on Mama's rock, and I pulled my knees to my chin and gazed into the road that had brought me to the village.

The sun was starting to dip. I looked up at the sky; there was no threat of rain. I thought that the sky looked exactly as it was on the day I first arrived at The Gate. I thought that the road which had brought me was silent in the same way. I thought that all things were exactly as they were on that first day. I sighed and looked into the road, wondering what it would bring. And as I looked, I saw a boy coming. When he got closer, I saw that he had no shirt and no shoes; just a pair of shorts. And he walked slowly, as if unsure whether to continue forward or to turn back.

He must have seen me for he walked with purpose now, heading in my direction. When he was close enough for me to make out his face, my heart started to beat uneasily. I rose to my feet and began to walk towards him until I was standing right in front of him and gazing down at his tired face. I began to tremble all over. I thought I must be in a dream. And in that state of a dream, all I could do was whisper his name, 'Noah.' Tears began to stream down my face.

He stared up at me, agony and fear in his eyes, and he shook his head.

'Noah,' I repeated, stretching forth my hands to touch his face, to ease his tiredness.

He shook his head again. 'My name is not Noah,' he said in a weak voice.

I ignored his words. 'My son, how did you get here?' I asked, leading him to sit on Mama's rock seeing that he was tired and disoriented.

I bent down before him, staring deep into his eyes. It was as if the dream in which I had found myself was growing more surreal by the seconds. 'How did you get here?' I asked again.

And then he spoke words that almost shattered the glass-like fragility of my surreal world. 'I don't have a name. Everyone calls me boy. I have no father or mother. I have no sister or brother. I have nobody. I have been wandering for longer than I can remember. I'm tired and hungry.' He began to cry.

His grief broke my heart. I embraced him tightly. 'Your name is Noah,' I said, in a trembling voice. 'You've been through a bad experience, which is why you have forgotten your name and your past. I'm your mother.

The Chief of our village kidnapped you. They were going to execute me, so I fled, leaving you behind. I'm so sorry that I left you behind. Please forgive me. I will take you to our new home.' I wept bitter tears.

'I'm hungry,' he said, his voice barely audible. 'I want food.'

'I will prepare you something to eat as soon as we get home,' I told him.

He nodded and took a few breaths, as if gasping for air.

*　*　*

I introduced him to the maids, and I insisted on cooking his food personally. While the food was cooking, I bathed him with warm water scented with herbal oils. He closed his eyes, drawing air deeply into his lungs, as if filling himself with a new life.

As I bathed him, a deep frown suddenly crossed my face. At first I could not tell why. And then I realised that the prominent birthmark that was on his upper back was no longer there. I wondered what had happened to it. Surely, it couldn't have disappeared just like that. I checked all over his body, hoping that for some reason it had shifted position, but I could not find it. I scrutinised his face. No doubt he was my son; two people could not look so alike, yet I felt troubled that I could not find the birthmark. Not wanting anything to spoil the joy of our reunion, I told myself that whatever had happened to the birthmark was irrelevant. It did not even matter that he had no recollection of his past. I knew this was a result of his traumatic experience. And it occurred to me that I would have to teach him all that he had forgotten. Thankfully, we had the whole time in the world.

When I finished bathing him, I rubbed Vaseline on his face and body, but he rubbed more on by himself, the way he liked to do. I laughed when I saw how oily his face was. To my great delight, he laughed, too. I wiped off the excess Vaseline with my palm. I felt very glad to see that he was already recovering well.

In one of the rooms, I found some clean clothes which were his size. And I found him a pair of slippers too. 'I'll get you new clothes and other things on the next market-day,' I told him, and he nodded.

The food was ready by now. I took him to the dining table and served him his favourite dish. By the time he finished eating his eyes were very heavy and he was starting to nod. In the bedroom, he promptly fell to sleep as soon as he dropped on the bed.

I had made up my mind that until he got accustomed to his new home, he was better off sharing my bedroom with me. So I had had to move in a smaller bed for him. Oyi and I sat on my bed, watching him sleep, listening to his gentle snoring.

'You never told us you had a son,' Oyi spoke quietly.

'That's because I was not so sure of his whereabouts,' I replied. 'He was kidnapped shortly before I ran away from my village, and I had to leave him behind because I was afraid for my life. Thankfully, he has managed to find me. He cannot remember much because of the trauma he had suffered. But I'm sure that in time, he will recollect all that he has forgotten.'

'He is such a brave little boy to have travelled all that distance to find you,' Oyi said wondrously. 'Powerful forces must have protected him on his journey. In our village, we believe that when a child is in search of the mother, that child is given special protection by the gods. That's what must have happened. The gods guided your son to you.'

'How I wish they would protect the innocent orphans in the same way,' I said, speaking my thought aloud.

We sat in silence.

After a while Oyi rose to her feet. 'I will leave now, I look forward to playing with Noah tomorrow,' she said and flashed her shy smile.

* * *

He woke up in the morning looking refreshed. He had slept soundly during the night, and I had spent most of that time watching over him. While he slept, questions had nibbled at my mind, but I pushed them all away, telling myself not to allow doubt to spoil the miracle of our reunion.

'Good morning, my son,' I greeted him with a smile, going over to sit on his bed. 'You're awake.'

He sat up and pulled the sheets to his chin. For a moment he stared at me with a frown, as if unsure where he was. And then he said, 'Good morning.'

I cuddled him together with the sheets, pressing my cheek against his. 'How are you feeling? Did you sleep well?' I asked.

He nodded. 'Yes, I slept well. I have never slept so well.'

'I'm so happy to hear that,' I said. And then

broadening my smile, I asked, 'How come you're not calling me Mother? That's what you call me — Mother.'

'Yes, Mother,' he said, with a nod.

I felt thrilled. 'Do you remember anything now, anything about the village where we used to live?' I asked, studying his face.

He frowned for a moment. 'No,' he said, shaking his head.

'Don't worry, you will remember everything. I will tell you all about our lives in the village where we used to live.'

'Okay, Mother.' He nodded.

'This is our new home,' I told him. 'Once you get used to it you will have your own room, across from mine. It's a very big house, and we have some very good people helping to take care of it. You met some of them yesterday. You will meet the others today. I'm sure everyone will like you.'

He beamed with delight. 'Can we take a look round?' he asked. And, suddenly coming alive, he pushed the sheets aside and jumped out of bed.

'Yes, come, I will show you!'

From that moment, he was like a child plugged to the source of happiness after a time of very sad experiences.

* * *

He enjoyed instant popularity in the house. When Oyi asked him how old he was, he turned to me. 'You're going to be nine soon,' I told him and he nodded. The age difference between him and the house helps notwithstanding, he related with them as if they were his new-found friends. He asked their names; he asked about their families, and he asked what they did when they were not working in the house. And he told them that I was his mother, but that he had forgotten everything about our lives in the village we used to live.

'Mother will teach me everything, and I will remember again,' he said.

He was so full of life that the house, which used to be very quiet, soon began to ring with voices and incessant laughter. It was as if his coming had woken the house out of an ancient slumber, and as if he came with a dozen friends. He wanted to know what everyone was doing at every point in time, and he offered to help, even if the task was more than he could handle. With him around, everyone was encouraged to work much harder. He came to be known as the little Master of the house and he showed a maturity and kindliness that belied his age. I realised, with great delight, that the bad experience he suffered had turned him into an even better child. He had always been a good boy, but now he exuded a vibrant personality that affected everyone with happiness.

It was Oyi who first took him into the village after a few days. He felt so thrilled to see children playing all around. Some were flying kites of different colours and sizes, others played games with snail shells in the sands. Soon, he broke away from Oyi and joined in a rowdy game of football. And he displayed such skills that warranted the other kids to gather round him when the game had ended. They told him he was a great player, and they asked who he was.

'My name is Noah,' he said. 'I live with my mother and some good people in the big house over there.' He pointed in the general direction of our house. 'I just arrived a few days ago to join my mother.'

The other kids introduced themselves. Among them was Ladu, who was about the same age as Noah; Bekes, who was slightly older; and Tudoh, who was older than all of them, but was smallest in size. They wanted to know where Noah learnt his skills and they asked if he cared to play with them every day.

'Yes, I would love to play with you every day,' he said, excited.

'Maybe you could teach us some of your skills,' Tudoh said.

'And you will teach me yours too,' Noah said. And then he turned to look at Oyi where she had been standing, watching their game. 'I have to leave now with my auntie, she's over there.' He pointed at Oyi.

'So we will see you tomorrow then?'

'Yes.' He waved at them and left with Oyi.

★ ★ ★

In under a week, the whole village was talking about Noah. Friends came to visit him at home, and they turned our large compound into their playground. They divided themselves into groups and engaged in all sorts of game that filled the air with delightful screams and so much dust.

In Oyi, Noah found a loving chaperon who cooked for him and his friends.

'Don't worry, Mother,' he would say to me, 'Auntie Oyi will take care of us.' And to Oyi, 'My friends will be tired and hungry at the end of our game. Please kindly get something ready for us to eat when we finish.' And Oyi would assure him with a smile that food would be on the table by the time they finish.

The dining room was big, but there weren't enough seats for all of them, so they sat on the floor. They preferred to sit on the floor because it gave them the freedom to eat and play by spinning their plates on the floor. The boy who spun his plate fastest without spilling its content was the champion, and they cheered him with great excitement.

'Boys, boys, it's not proper to eat and talk and play at the same time!' Oyi would announce loudly, standing with her hands on her hips in the doorway. For a few moments, silence would prevail. But as soon as she turned her back, they chattered more animatedly than before, as if her interruption had been designed to fire their excitement.

At the end of each day, it often took several announcements from Oyi to get the boys to go back home. Sometimes, not until she had threatened that whoever got out last would not be allowed into the compound the next day. And then they would scramble to make it to the exit ahead of the others, waving their hands behind them in farewell to Noah.

*   *   *

Every evening, I encouraged him to tell me about his new-found friends when we were seated by the lantern. I purposely avoided mentioning anything about the village of our origin because I wanted him to settle into his new life before taking him on a journey to the past.

But one evening he surprised me by asking, 'Where is my father, Mother? And where are my brothers and sisters?'

We were sitting alone in the living room. For a few moments I closed my eyes and said a silent prayer, asking for wisdom to answer his question.

'Mother?' he said, bending his head to look up at me.

And then I began to tell him a story I had once heard, about a man who had died in search of happiness. 'Your father was a very good man,' I said and paused. 'And he loved us so much. But the world was a very sad place at that time. So your father decided to go in search of happiness so that he could share it with you and me. He discovered happiness, but he died in the process. But before he died, he told us the secret of happiness. And it is that secret that makes us very happy today.' I smiled warmly at him.

'And what is that secret, Mother?' he asked, curious.

'The secret is that we must always be happy even if the whole world is sad,' I said. 'That is the secret of happiness which your father passed to us. And as long as we keep that secret, we will always find happiness.'

'What if you're sad, how do you keep the secret of happiness?'

'That is the big secret! You must never allow yourself to be sad. Instead, you must always make yourself happy no matter how sad things may be. That is the big secret which most people do not know.'

'So I must not be sad that Pa is dead?' he asked.

'Exactly! You must not be sad because you have the secret of happiness.'

He nodded his head slowly, saying nothing. Then he asked, 'What about my brothers and sisters? Do I have any?'

'Your father and I had only you because we wanted to give you the best in life. But you don't have to worry, you have many good friends. Your friends are your brothers and sisters, too.'

He nodded. 'And I will teach them the secret of happiness,' he said quietly.

'I'm proud of you, my son,' I said, pulling him to me. 'You're very strong.'

★　★　★

The next day, I received a surprise visit from the High Priest while Noah was out playing. It was the first time I would see the man since I had arrived in the village. He was a big and tall man, dressed in a red gown that reached his feet, and he wore several red beads around his neck that seemed to weigh him down. In his right hand he carried a short broom. When he introduced himself, fire seemed to spit out of his mouth. No doubt, he was a powerful man.

But he gave me a very friendly smile, and this surprised me. I invited him to take a seat. Oyi quickly brought a calabash of water for him, and she knelt before him until he had finished drinking. He returned the calabash to her and prayed for her, and she started to retreat from the living room. Not wanting to be left alone with the man, I called her back. 'We have an important visitor,' I said. 'I think you should stay while he is around, in case he needs something.'

She understood why I had called her back. She nodded and stood in a corner of the living room with her head bowed, holding the calabash in both hands. I could see her looking at me from the corner of her eye, a faint smile playing on her lips.

'Where is the boy?' the High Priest asked abruptly, his friendly smile gone.

I looked at Oyi, who nodded imperceptibly. 'He is out playing,' I said.

'News got to me that you have a boy living with you, but no one knows where he came from. Is he an orphan?'

My heart began to beat fast. 'He is my son,'

I said sharply, 'not an orphan.'

'When you came you did not tell anyone you had a son. And before Mama died, she mentioned that you would be coming, not that your son would be coming to join you. Where did the boy come from?' he asked, as if giving me a final opportunity to tell the truth. 'Is he really your son?'

I thought of the missing birthmark. How could he be my son without the birthmark? How could he not be my son? Could two people look so much alike? How come he doesn't remember anything about his past — me, his father, our village, his friends? I asked myself these silent questions. For the umpteenth time, I told myself that they did not matter.

'He came from the village where we used to live,' I said. 'It's a village far away from here, about one month's journey by foot. I left him behind when I ran away. He followed me to be with me. He is my son; his name is Noah.'

'I know his name. We all know his name. You want me to believe that he is your son? How could a mere child make a journey of that distance alone?'

'The gods must have protected him and led him to his mother,' Oyi spoke quietly, her eyes on the floor.

The High Priest fixed his eyes on Oyi for a moment. Finally, he rose to his feet. 'It's my duty to tell you that in our village no one is allowed to take in an orphan except they are maternal relatives of the child,' he said.

'I know, the tradition is the same where I come from,' I said. 'The boy is my son, not an orphan.'

The High Priest pursed his lips. 'I must leave now,' he said. 'At the right time, the Chief may want to know exactly why you ran away from your village.' Waving his broom in the air, he chanted quiet incantations as he left.

For several moments, Oyi and I remained silent. And then she asked, 'Why exactly did you run away from your village?' Her voice was a whisper.

I remembered Mama's warning. I knew I could not tell her the truth. 'I ran away because of love,' I said. I could not say more without telling her the truth.

'What about love?' she asked.

'Because I could not fall in love,' I said, not knowing what to say.

She sensed that I was afraid to tell her the truth. So she helped me. 'If you ran away because you were being compelled to marry someone you don't love, then that is a good reason. In our village, tradition does not compel you to marry someone you don't love. Love is a matter of choice. So if you ran away because of love, then we are obliged to grant you refuge.'

'Yes, I ran away because I was being compelled to marry another man.'

She nodded encouragingly at me. 'Say no more than that,' she said.

* * *

Following the High Priest's visit, it occurred to me that I must help Noah remember all that he had forgotten as a matter of urgency. So that night, I told him a lot more about our village of origin, of the things that he had forgotten. I told him about our house, and our small farm in the backyard which had a barn in which we stored our harvests. I told him of his cousins Loko and Luku, of his experience when he was taken away from me to live with his uncle Jaja. And I told him of Kpofe, his father's best friend who lived in the city, and the role he played to help me regain his custody. But I did not tell him of his four friends on the outskirts. I felt that it was not yet time to remind him of that crucial part of our lives.

He was intrigued. He asked many questions; my answers carried him on a journey into his forgotten past, late into the night. The oil in the lantern dried up and the light went out. I filled the lantern with more oil, and when I lit it the flame flared brightly, causing him to jump with fright, and then he laughed.

I told him of my position as a foremost trader on Main Street and how his father used to supply me vegetables which I sold to the merchants who came to our market. And then the rains came and destroyed our market and farms. And a harsh famine came upon the land. I told him about Chair-Lady. And I told him about the eponymous painting which the late High Priest said would be the key to a great destiny one day. 'I believe that you will come across that painting one day,' I said. 'In the painting, you will see me standing in the middle of our market, and you will see how busy it used to be, before the rain destroyed everything.'

I covered a great part of our lives, and he listened attentively. And then he began to yawn, and I knew that it was time for us to go to bed. I led him to his room — now he had his own room, just across from mine. When he had climbed into bed, I kissed him goodnight. As I turned to go, he held my hand.

And he said, 'Mother, I would love to become a merchant one day so that I can travel to distant lands to do business. I like the way merchants conduct their business. They are hard-working and they command a lot of respect.'

I smiled to myself. I had always known that he would pursue a great destiny. 'It's a good dream, my son,' I said, sitting on the bed. 'It's a very good dream. You see, I have been thinking about opening a small provision shop in front of our house, by the gate. Now that you have told me of your dream, I will open it very soon and we will run it together so you can learn the principles of trading. With what you will learn, you can become a great merchant and travel the world one day.'

'Thank you, Mother,' he said and promptly fell asleep.

I sat there for a while. I watched him as he slept, snoring gently. Then I rose and left the room with the lantern. I could see a bright future for my son.

14

In the weeks that followed, we built a small shop by the gate. Soluso and Kewe carried out the job. When they had finished, I inspected it, and it was exactly what I wanted. There was enough room inside the shop for two people to sit down. Outside, the zinc roofing extended outward providing shade for customers while they collected their shopping through a window which served as a counter.

While the construction of the shop was ongoing, Oyi and I had travelled to a town a few hours away to make arrangements with a merchant who would be supplying me with provisions. We made the journey on a rickety bus which plied that route every market-day. I had never taken a bus before. I enjoyed the experience, but the sound of the engine sounded very loud to my ears.

It was the first time I would travel to any town. I was amazed how big it was. I saw a great multitude. I saw sights that turned my senses upside down, and I felt like an alien as I gawked. The people I bumped into simply shrugged me aside and continued on their way in a hurry. I wondered where they were headed to in such hurry; I could not imagine what was waiting for them at their ultimate destinations. The strident sounds in the air filled me with a sense of fear and urgency, and I thought that if I stayed in the town for just one night I would wake up in the morning a different person. This thought made me very uncomfortable, and I told myself that we must get back to the village as soon as possible.

Oyi had been to the town on one or two occasions before. She seemed very much at ease; so I thought. She told me the population of the town was about five thousand people. I wondered how so many people could live in one place. The merchant we came to see told us a great deal about the town, and he said that the city was even far bigger than the town.

'How big is the city?' I asked the merchant, thinking about Kpofe.

'Ah, the city is very big,' he said, 'too big to count the people who live there. The city will swallow twenty towns or more.'

His answer sent my head spinning, and I realised that I had no chance of finding Kpofe if I ever went to the city.

We negotiated with the merchant to be delivering provisions to my store once a month. He made a list of the items that I requested. It was a long list, from sweets to candles and bread. He assured me that he would make sure that I received my supply regularly through his distributor. I paid in advance for the first delivery, and we caught the bus back to the village.

★　★　★

After weeks of meticulous planning and hard work, we finally opened for business. It was a joyous occasion for Noah and me, and for everyone. Noah brought his friends to witness the opening ceremony. The boys took turns to go into the shop to admire it. They came out awed at all the items they had seen on display. There were only two of such shops in the whole of the village, and they were much smaller than our own. Everyone came to witness the opening ceremony, which was conducted by the Chief, and they all found something that they could buy.

That first day, business was very good. It surprised me that Noah did not go to play with his friends, even though I said he could go. Instead, he stayed with me and helped to attend to the customers who thronged the shop. When his friends came to call him, he begged them to excuse him, that he would join them some other time. They showed great understanding and went into the village to play without him. I was impressed with his attitude. Already, he had begun to display the qualities of a great merchant.

We were exhausted at the close of business that first day. After we had taken a bath and eaten, we sat in the living room, each nursing a cup of sweet local beverage made from millet, which Oyi had prepared for us.

'It has been a good first day; you have done very well.' I smiled at Noah.

'Thank you, Mother,' he said. 'I'm going to learn so much from you. When I become a merchant, I will buy the kind of coat and hat merchants wear.'

'I'm sure you will.' Oyi laughed, patting Noah on the head. 'I was really amazed at the number of customers that came today,' she said. 'It's a surprise how the two of you managed to cope.'

'That's business,' I said. 'You have to learn to cope.' I had told Oyi and the others that the business would be managed strictly by Noah and me.

'Now I understand what you mean when you said you were a foremost trader in your former village.' Oyi said and laughed.

'Back then I learnt to stand on my feet for

hours on end, attending to one customer or the other. And even when there were no customers to attend to, I stayed on my feet because I had gotten used to standing. It's part of business. It keeps you on your toes.'

'Mother, I think we should have regular opening and closing times,' Noah spoke suddenly, holding his drink in both hands and leaning forward.

I smiled to myself, impressed. 'I was going to discuss that with you,' I said. 'It's important to have specific opening and closing times in business.'

He nodded, sipping his drink, waiting for me to continue.

'In the morning, we will open the shop soon after breakfast. And then we will close for about an hour for lunch. After lunch, we open again until the sun starts to go down, then we close for the day,' I explained.

'What if we go on lunch break in shifts?' Noah asked. 'It means that the shop will be open to customers for longer hours.'

Again he had impressed me. I nodded. 'It's a good idea, in fact, that's the way a business should be run, but I want us to have our meals together. Meal-times are important. So we close for lunch at the same time and open again after we have eaten. All we need to do is advise our customers about our opening and closing hours. Or we could hang a sign on the door.'

'I think the sign will work well,' he said and yawned.

'One last thing before we go to sleep,' I said. 'I can see you are sleepy.'

He nodded. 'What's that, Mother?'

'I don't want you to take part in the business fulltime.'

'Why not?' he asked, sitting up.

'Because I want you to have time to play with your friends. At your age, you should work and play in equal measure. So you must always make time to play with your friends. We could do it two ways — either you work fulltime with me every other day and use your off days to play with your friends, or you work every day but close at lunchtime and have the rest of the day to yourself. Which do you prefer?'

He thought for a moment. 'I think I will work every other day,' he said.

'So that settles it,' I said.

Oyi had been listening to us quietly. 'I think this business is going to be very successful the way you are going about it,' she said, quite impressed.

'I pray so,' I said.

Noah yawned again.

It had been a long day. We finished our drinks and retired to bed.

★ ★ ★

On his first day off, Noah did not get to play much with his friends because they gathered around him and asked him questions about our shop.

'I'm going to be a merchant one day,' he told them. 'My mother is teaching me how to trade. When I become a merchant I will travel to far places and bring new things to our village.'

The boys were excited. Some said they wanted to be farmers, others said they wanted to be fishermen because fishermen are known to be very rich. One boy said he wanted become a bus driver so that he could travel to the city and see the wonders that existed there.

'I want to become a politician,' Bekes said. 'And I will make laws that will transform our village into a city.'

'How can you become a politician when you have not been to school?' Tudoh said. 'You're dreaming a dream that is too big for you.'

'No dream is too big for me!' Bekes snapped. 'I will go the city one day, like our new Chief did. And I will go to school when I get to the city. And then I will become a politician. You will see.'

'My mother said you can become anything you want to be,' Noah said. 'But she also said that you have to work for it. I'm sure that we can all become what we want to become.'

'I want to become Chief one day,' Tudoh said. 'Me, I want to remain in the village. I don't want to go to the city or any far away land. I want to stay here and become Chief. And all of you will bring me presents and bow before me.'

A fierce argument broke out. 'We are not going to bow before you!' Bekes snapped. 'Who are you that we would bow before you, tiny as you are?'

'I will be Chief,' Tudoh said calmly.

Several boys chased him, wanting to beat him to show him that he could never rule over them. He ran very fast on spindly legs and they could not catch up with him. So they turned back panting, and continued to dream about their own futures. Bekes' vision, which is to transform their village into a city, fired their imagination most.

★　★　★

There were times when business was so slow we would not see a single customer in many

217

hours. I used such times to tell Noah more stories about the village of our birth. And, eventually, I told myself that it was time to tell him the origin of the dream that we shared there, a dream which earned me the death penalty and forced me to flee.

I realised that it was my duty to tell him the origin of that dream exactly as it had been. It was what gave meaning to all our struggles, even our existence. So I took my time to tell the story so that he could relive it as we had lived it then. I saw in his eyes that his memory was being rekindled. And I knew that it was just a matter of time before we began to dream that ancient dream all over again. Even as Mama had told me, I felt certain that this was both of our destinies. I had seen so many things by now to know what destiny was. And I had enjoyed so many blessings, enough to know that we could only live the fullness of our destiny by becoming a blessing to others.

I began by telling him about the evil tradition of our village which labelled orphans evil children. I told him of their plight and how they often end up in the abandoned building on the outskirts, the halfway house from where they travel to distant lands never to return. I told him of the day the old chief had convened a meeting at which he spelt out my rights and obligations as a widow. And how, when we got back home, he, Noah, had told me of his encounter with four orphan boys when he had gone to pluck mango with his neighbourhood friends on the outskirts against my wish.

And so the story slowly unfolded.

He did not ask questions; he just listened. I could tell that his emotions were the same as they had been all that time ago. I could tell also that he felt the same way about the orphans as he had then. And I saw a kindness in his eyes that reminded me of his father.

★ ★ ★

I had forgotten what it was like to be in love. I had left that feeling behind in the village of my birth. But I soon discovered that Kewe was trying to revive that feeling in me. He brought me fruits often. And now that I worked in the shop fulltime, he would stay by the window which served as a counter and engage me in chit-chat when there were no customers around. He was a very witty young man, and very good looking too. But it was not about him; I could no longer feel the beat of love in my heart.

'I'm a widow,' I said to him and laughed, 'a

widow who no longer submits to the longings of the heart.'

It was Noah's off day. There was no customer around. Kewe stood outside the window chatting to me. He had brought me a bunch of banana and some oranges. I peeled some of the oranges and passed a couple to him through the window. I watched him suck his orange. I liked the way he sucked his orange, as if it was the sweetest thing in the world. I finished sucking an orange and I ate a banana. I had put some away for Noah. Kewe always came on Noah's off day, and I always kept some of the fruits he brought for Noah. Now, as we chatted, it occurred to me that I was developing a fondness for Kewe, but it had nothing to do with love. The only man I had ever loved was Tanto. Of course, I no longer knew what it meant to be in love.

'But you're a very beautiful widow,' Kewe said.

'Thank you,' I said. 'That's what everybody says, but it does not make me special or better than any other person.'

'I think you're special,' he said. 'And I think I like you a lot.'

'I like you a lot too,' I said, 'not because you're good looking but because you have a kind heart.'

'That's such a nice thing to say.' He smiled.

For a few moments we were silent. 'You work too hard,' he said. 'You need to do other things.'

'Well, work keeps me busy and I enjoy what I do.'

'Still, you must take time off now and then. I want to take you out,' he said.

'Take me where?' I asked.

'To The Gate to watch the sun set. It's very beautiful out there.'

'I know, I have been there a few times. That was where I met Mama when I first arrived here. And it was where my son found me when he came in search of me. The Gate is a very special place for me.'

'I would like to take you there tomorrow. Maybe you could close early? Please don't say no.' He smiled.

His smile was charming. 'It wouldn't be a bad idea,' I said.

*   *   *

We went to The Gate the next evening. We got there just before the sun began to sink behind the horizon. There was no one about. I sat on Mama's rock and Kewe sat on another, close to me. A gentle breeze was blowing. I looked into the road that had brought me, and then Noah, to the village and I smiled, grateful that the road was there.

The sun was a shimmering orange ball. We watched it with fascination. And as we did, it suddenly disappeared then appeared again, as if playing a trick on us. I smiled. We watched for many minutes, following which the sun began its final descent. Now it was a ball of many fiery but subtle colours blending together. A dark cloud slowly encroached on its edge, swallowing it up. And darkness promptly fell upon the world.

We turned to look at each other with faint smiles.

'It is such a beautiful sight, isn't it?' Kewe said.

I just nodded, saying nothing.

In that silence we sat for a while. Strangely, the sky seemed to brighten a little even though darkness had fallen. The road was empty. But I knew that one day it would take my son back home to his roots, and I knew that when that time came I would have fulfilled my destiny. I smiled and blew the road a kiss.

My mind suddenly went to Bomboi and the others, but I did not think of them in a sad way. 'I understand that orphans are treated badly here,' I said.

'It has been like that for ages. It is tradition,' Kewe replied.

'It's an evil tradition,' I said quietly.

'I agree with you, but there's nothing any of us can do about it.'

'Only because nobody wants to do anything about it.'

'Mama tried to, but the chief at that time and the people resisted it.'

'Let me ask you, would you want to see that tradition change?'

'Of course I would!' Kewe said. 'Some of us would love to see it change. The new chief is doing things differently. Maybe things will change during his reign. Everyone is afraid of the priests. But I'm hopeful even that will change one day.'

I nodded at his optimism. We walked on in silence for a while.

'Do you have a girlfriend?' I asked, suddenly.

'Yes,' he replied. 'But I like you in a way I cannot explain.' He reached for my hand and pulled me to my feet. 'Let's go back.'

We walked back to the village slowly.

'Come with your girlfriend to the shop tomorrow,' I said. 'I would like to meet her.'

'Okay, I will do so. But don't forget that I like you in a really special way. Honestly, I do.'

'I know. It's called friendship,' I said and laughed.

Her name was Chamuke. She was a very pretty girl. And I could tell that she was very shy, too. I came out of the shop to greet them. I remembered that I had seen her on a few occasions before, even on the day I opened the shop, when the whole village had come. I remember seeing her and thinking that she was a very pretty girl. I was not surprised; she and Kewe were a perfect match.

After we had greeted, I said to her, 'Your boyfriend and I are good friends.'

She nodded. 'I know,' she said and smiled. 'He talks about you always. I was jealous at first. But not anymore.'

'Good, I'm glad to hear that. I hope you will come to see me often.'

'Yes, I will.' She nodded and then said, 'I see Noah around a lot. He is such a lovely boy, far bigger than others his age. He told me he is eight, but he looks twelve.' She laughed.

'I'm surprised myself the way he is growing,' I said.

'It's good,' Kewe said. 'He is going to be a big strong man, like me.'

'No, like his father,' I said and we all laughed.

They took their leave when customers began to trickle in.

And then it was time for lunch. I closed the shop when Oyi came to inform me that lunch was ready. To my surprise, Noah was not at home for lunch. He was always there for lunch; he knew when to come.

'Where is Noah?' I asked Oyi.

'I'm surprised he has not shown up,' she said. 'He must be on his way.'

'I will wait for him to come.'

'You go ahead and eat.' Soluso said. 'I will go and find him.'

I had almost finished eating when Noah turned up with Soluso. 'I'm sorry that I'm late, Mother,' he said grinning broadly. 'My side was losing a game and I had to make sure I scored a goal before leaving.'

'So did you score the goal?' I asked.

'Yes, I did, and my side won!'

'Go and wash your hands and come and eat,' I said, smiling

Soon he came to join me at the table. He was still eating when I went to reopen the shop.

★ ★ ★

Business was very good.

At the end of our first month of trading, I

225

returned to the town with Oyi to renegotiate my contract with the merchant.

The merchant was delighted to see us and to hear that business was going well. He entertained us with cold Fanta and biscuits. The drink was so cold I felt a chill right from my head all the way down to my feet and it was as if my brain had stopped functioning for a moment or two. The Fanta I sold in the village was never cold because I had no fridge and even if I had had a fridge, there was no electricity to power it. So I sold warm Fanta to my customers, who drank it like that and liked it. But cold Fanta was a totally different experience. I promised myself that once electricity came to our village, I would buy a fridge to sell cold Fanta and Coke.

After I had renewed my contract, Oyi and I strolled through the town. I was not yet at ease like Oyi, but I was starting to get used to the town a bit. As we went, I noticed children in uniform carrying books. Oyi explained that they were just finishing school. 'One day they will grow up to be lawyers and doctors and politicians,' she said.

As I watched the children an idea suddenly came to me. 'We could have a school in our village, too,' I said, excited. 'And our children too could become great one day.'

'What are you talking about?' Oyi asked.

I did not answer her. I just pulled her along, the idea growing in my mind.

15

Time passed and I forgot that orphans existed in the village. I forgot about the brilliant idea for a school that had come to me when I visited the town with Oyi. I forgot about so many things; only my son and my business mattered to me. And I started to drift, like you drift when life becomes monotonous.

And then I went to shop alone one market-day, and I bumped into Bisco, the young merchant who did business in the village of my birth, and often boasted of his journeys to the big city. I could not believe my eyes. I stood before him, peering at him as if I had been blind and had suddenly recovered my sight but was not sure if I was seeing right. For a long moment, he peered at me also, disbelief in his eyes. And then, raising his hand to his mouth, he whispered my name, 'Ese.' He nodded his head, as if to assure himself that it really was me. 'Ese,' he said again.

'Bisco!' I cried, reaching out my hand until I was almost touching his face. And then we both shouted with great delight and rushed into each other's arms in a warm embrace.

'Is it really you, Bisco?' I asked after we had broken apart.

'Yes, it is me!' And then looking deep into my eyes, he said, 'I'm so sorry about everything that happened to you. I visited your village to see if business had picked up, but it hadn't. Chair-Lady told me all that happened. I'm so sorry.' He shook his head.

Several curious onlookers had gathered around us by now. Afraid that he would say something that could expose my secrets, I took his hand and led him urgently through the market to a quiet spot.

'What was it Chair-Lady told you?' I asked.

He sighed. 'She told me how your son died and of your involvement with the orphans, and the death penalty being imposed on you.'

'My son did not die!' I spoke fiercely, keeping my voice to a whisper. 'It was a lie made up by the Chief because I refused to marry him. My son lives in this village with me now.'

A look of confusion spread across his face. 'But everyone I spoke with in the village told me the same thing,' he said.

'I told you, it was all a lie made up by the Chief,' I snapped.

The look on his face deepened. He shrugged. And then he jolted me with his next words. 'I saw Kpofe in the city,' he said.

I screamed with joy. 'You saw him?' I looked round to make sure that nobody was paying attention to us. 'You saw Kpofe?' I asked.

'Yes.'

'How? Where did you see him?' I asked.

He shook his head slowly, as if lost for words.

'What is it?' I asked.

'I saw him in the wholesale market where I usually go to buy goods. He came there to look for a job.'

'I thought he had a job in the city?'

'He told me that he lost his job. He told me he lost his girlfriend, too. He looked very unhappy.'

'I thought they were going to get married? What happened?' I could not hide the anguish in my voice.

'He didn't say.' Bisco replied. 'I begged my friend who owned a shop in the market to give him a job. It is the biggest market in the city. He works there now.'

I stayed silent, my heart beating unevenly, and I wondered why things had gone so wrong for Kpofe.

'It's my first time in this market.' I heard Bisco's voice, as if from a distance. 'I just came to see it. I may come to do business here one day.'

'When are you next going to the city?' I asked.

'I don't know, maybe in two weeks' time.'

'When you go, please tell Kpofe I live here now. Tell him I had to leave our village.'

'I will tell him.'

'Bisco . . . ' I said hesitantly.

'Yes.' He leaned closer to me.

'Nobody in this village must know anything about me, anything about what Chair-Lady told you.'

He nodded. 'I understand,' he said, pursing his lips.

I managed a weak smile. I left the market and returned home, saddened by the news I had received.

★ ★ ★

I did not mention my encounter with Bisco to Noah because I did not want him to know about Kpofe's tough times in the city.

In the following days, I agonised over Kpofe's fate. I wept silently for him, and I prayed that Bisco would go to the city soon and deliver my message to him. I wondered if he would come to visit Noah and I. Suddenly, I hated the city for what it had done to Kpofe. And I came to understand what he meant when he said the city was a difficult place when you have no job. But I remembered him telling me that God in heaven answers prayers. So I prayed for him, hoping that things would get better for him.

Not long after, just when I had begun to wonder if God had answered my prayer for Kpofe, Noah encountered an orphan.

It was his day off. He had gone out early because Ladu wanted to show him how to prepare a fishing line. On his way to Ladu's house, he passed a rubbish dump. And to his surprise, he saw a boy about his age scavenging for food. The boy looked very thin. He began to move away when he saw Noah approaching, as if he had been caught in a criminal act.

'What are you doing?' Noah asked, surprised to see the boy carrying a bowl which contained some of the items he had dug from the rubbish. He had never seen the boy before, and he wondered if he was from the village.

The boy continued to retreat backwards in slow steps, holding the bowl close to his chest. Noah walked towards him. And then the boy turned and began to run and Noah pursued him without thinking. Soon he caught up with the boy because he was much stronger. The boy stopped running, panting and cowering in the presence of Noah.

'What were you doing there?' Noah asked, reaching out to touch the boy gently.

The boy looked up, saying nothing.

'I'm not going to hurt you,' Noah said. 'I'm a boy like you. I won't hurt you. I just want to know what you were doing there'

'I was looking for food to eat,' the boy replied. He had begun to relax a little because Noah was a boy. If it were an adult, he would have run without stopping.

'Don't you have food to eat at home?'

'No.'

'Why not?' Noah asked, surprised.

'Because I'm an orphan,' the boy replied.

'And where do you live?'

'I live with my uncle, my late mother's brother. They say I'm bad. They beat me and they don't give me food most times. So I go to the rubbish dump to get something to eat.'

Noah felt deflated, and for several moments he did not know what to say. 'Come with me,' he said finally. 'I will take you to my house and my mother will get you something to eat.'

★ ★ ★

I was surprised when Noah showed up with him at the shop.

'Mother, this is my friend, Bobo. He says

233

he is an orphan and he has not had anything to eat for days. I brought him home so that auntie Oyi can prepare some food for him to eat.' His voice was sad.

My heart began to race. I said nothing. I rose and led Noah and the boy out of the shop. Then I locked up and we went into the house. In the living room, holding the boy by the shoulders, I bent down to study his face. He looked thin and pale and it was obvious that he had endured great hardship, worse than the orphans in the village of my birth. I just stared into his face, unable to say a word. I could not believe that a child could be in such a pitiable condition in a village that was so peaceful and prosperous.

Oyi came into the living room. She took in the situation, and a deep sigh escaped her. I did not need to explain anything to her. I rushed to get the boy some banana and groundnuts and water, and I told Noah to keep him company while I went to the kitchen to cook yam for him.

Oyi followed me. 'I know the boy,' she said, 'he is an orphan. His name is Bobo. He has a younger sister called Ada, who is about six. They both live with their uncle.'

'And how is his sister?' I asked, looking up from what I was doing, my heart beating unpleasantly. 'How is she being treated?'

'The same way they treat the boy.'

'You mean she is in the same state?' My voice was faint.

'She is even worse. She is a girl, younger than the boy; she cannot endure as much as him. I see her every now and then. She is the most beautiful girl I have ever seen. After both of their parents died, they said she was a witch because she was so beautiful, that she killed her parents and passed some of her evil power to her brother. They had wanted to kill her, but they spared her because they believed she would confess one day. Then she can be sentenced to death. So they're waiting for the day she would confess.'

'Can you bring her to me, please?'

'I could try,' Oyi said uncertainly. 'It could cause a lot of problem for us if their family discover that they have been here.'

'Please don't think about that,' I said urgently. 'See if you can bring her here. Today. If possible, now.'

'Let me go to their house and see if I can get her here,' Oyi said.

★   ★   ★

I had finished boiling the yam and Bobo was eating at the table when Oyi walked in with Ada. My heart broke at the first sight of her.

She looked so thin, so frail, so beautiful — more beautiful than Oyi had described. I had never seen any child as beautiful as she was. In spite of the fact that she endured so much suffering, she looked like an angel — a persecuted angel. She had silent tears in her eyes. When she saw her brother, she began to cry loudly. She ran to him at the table, and she flung her arms around his neck.

Bobo had stopped eating. The yam in his hand had dropped on the table when he saw his sister. He struggled to swallow the food in his mouth. 'She is my sister,' he said to no one and began to cry loudly too. Noah started to cry too. I could not help myself and I allowed my tears to flow freely. And I just stood rooted on one spot, wishing that the nightmare would dissolve before my eyes.

Oyi tried to console all of us, begging us not to cry. She was very strong, Oyi. I could see in her eyes that she had tears in her soul, but she managed to contain them. She kept moving from one to the other, begging us not to cry, wiping our faces with her palms.

Finally, I dried my tears. Gently, I pulled Ada and Bobo apart. I wiped their faces with a clean cloth. And I got them to sit at the table. I brought more yam and palm oil for them, and I begged them to eat. They ate, looking at each other now and then. And then

Bobo smiled weakly at her. She smiled back at him.

I turned my face away, too sad to watch them in their innocence, knowing that their plight was a shame to society, to the human race.

Noah sat next to Ada at the table. He took her hand as she ate. 'Please you must never cry again,' he said. 'You are my friend and my sister. And Bobo is my friend and my brother.' He paused, then continued. 'Don't worry, I have the secret of happiness. I will share it with you both and we will live happily for ever.'

Ada smiled sweetly at him. She swallowed the food in her mouth. And she said, 'Thank you.'

'Eat your food,' Noah said, still holding her hand.

She nodded, and continued to eat. Now and then she turned to look at Bobo and then at Noah. And then she would smile.

After they had finished eating, Oyi and I retreated quietly from the room, leaving the three of them to get to know each other.

*　★　★

'They have to go back home before the family start looking for them,' Oyi said a few hours later.

'I want them to live with me. I don't want them to go back there,' I said. 'I cannot bear to let them go back. What can I do?' My voice was hopeless.

Oyi shook her head slowly. 'It would be impossible for them to live here with you. You heard what the High Priest said when he came. Moreover, their uncle will not allow them to live with you.'

'But they're being treated so badly! What's the point having them under his roof when they're not being properly cared for?'

'It's tradition. Tradition says they can only live with their maternal relatives. Look, let me take them back. They can come here secretly to eat, and you will still be able to look after them. But they must always go back home.'

'Where they live is not home,' I said. 'I could give them a home here.'

'I understand. Let's take it a step at a time. Maybe one day they will be able to live here with you.'

After a few moments of silence, I said, 'You may take them back.'

They became very sad when Oyi told them it was time to take them home. 'I will come and get you again tomorrow,' she said, but her words did nothing to brighten them. I could not bear to watch them. I retreated from the room and left the shop closed for the day.

It was the last time I would see Ada.

★   ★   ★

That night I tossed and turned in bed, unable to sleep. Their tearful faces kept flashing across my mind. I told myself that I would have to go and see the Chief and make my case before him. Somehow, I must take them into my custody. I was encouraged by Mama's dream that one day her house would be a refuge for orphans. I could never have peace again knowing that the poor kids were being treated worse than slaves. I thought of how beautiful Ada looked in spite of all that she had been through. I remembered how she had embraced her brother at the table. I knew that I must do something.

Finally, I managed to sleep but it was a fitful sleep. I was glad when morning came, hopeful that I would see them again. I rose early and went to check on Noah in his room. To my surprise he was up and had already taken his bath and dressed. He smiled and got up to hug me when I walked into his room. 'Good morning, Mother,' he said.

'Good morning, my son,' I said and smiled weakly. 'You are up early.'

Seeing the smile on my son's face dispelled some of the sadness in me. I felt very proud of him that he was truly keeping the secret of happiness. It was I who had given him that secret. I told myself that I must not fail to keep it. I could not afford to let him know that what I told him was a mere tale about a man who had died in the search of happiness.

'Yes, Mother,' he said sitting on the bed. 'Ada and Bobo would be coming to visit us again today.'

'Yes, they will be coming. I look forward to seeing them,' I said. 'Let me go and use the bathroom, and then we will have breakfast.'

'Okay, Mother,' he replied.

I patted him on the head and went out to wash.

★ ★ ★

I had just finished dressing up when I heard someone wailing in a loud voice. I stood still for a brief moment, and then I rushed out of my room into the yard to see what was amiss. Noah had rushed out of his room too. To my surprise, I discovered that it was Oyi, and she was sitting in a heap on the bare floor. I bent down to hold her, my heart beating uncontrollably. 'What's the matter?' I asked, trying to get her to stop crying. 'Talk to me, please,' I begged her.

'They killed her,' she said. 'They killed her.'

'Killed who?' I asked fearfully.

Still crying, she managed to explain. 'I learnt this morning that when they got home yesterday, they were beaten and tortured for coming here. The girl did not survive. Ada is dead. She's deadoooooooo!' she wailed.

I joined Oyi in a heap on the floor. 'What are you saying?' I asked, dazed. 'What do you mean Ada is dead?' A loud sound was echoing in my head and I was unaware that my face was wet with tears.

'They have killed Ada,' she said panting, placing her hands on her breast.

I closed my eyes, but tears kept streaming down my face. I sat there with Oyi in a heap. I had never known that it was possible to cry in heartbreak with a hopeless smile on one's face.

*　*　*

It was Noah who acted as my rock in those wretched hours.

'Mother, we have the secret of happiness, remember?' he said.

'I remember, my son,' I said, smiling sadly at him. 'Yes, we have the secret of happiness.'

'And you said we must always be happy

241

even if the whole world is sad, remember?'

'Yes, my son, I remember. And now that the whole world is sad we must be happy because we have the secret of happiness,' I said and nodded.

We sat in silence.

'Bobo is still alive,' he said, 'you must do something before anything bad happens to him. You must do something, Mother.' His voice was urgent. For the first time since the news of Ada's death broke that day, he began to cry.

And then it occurred to me that truly Bobo could suffer the same fate as his sister. I came out of my grief and pulled Noah to me. 'I will do something, my son. Nothing bad will happen to Bobo. I promise you, I will do something.'

He stopped crying and wiped his face. 'Thank you, Mother,' he said.

By late afternoon, Oyi came in with food for us, but we both told her that we did not feel like eating anything. Saying nothing, she took the food silently back to the kitchen and returned a moment later.

'Have you heard anything about Bobo?' I asked Oyi.

'No, I haven't. All I know is that he is alive. He survived the beating.'

'I want to go and see the Chief,' I said rising up.

One of the men who helped me around the house appeared at the door. 'You have a visitor,' he said and moved aside to let Kewe in. Soluso followed closely behind him.

'I'm sorry about the girl,' Kewe said, his voice trembling.

'I'm going to see the Chief,' I told him. 'It's time to do something. It's time to change the evil tradition that allows innocent orphans to be treated as slaves. Not one more orphan must die in this village.'

'I will go with you,' Kewe said.

'No, I will go alone.'

'We will support you,' Kewe said.

'Yes, we will all support you and convince others too,' Soluso said. 'While you go to see the Chief, we will go into the village to mobilise people. Kewe and I are youth leaders in the village and we have had a discussion. We are ready to stand up to the priests if you will take the lead.'

'Tell me,' I said. 'How many more orphans are there in this village?'

They consulted amongst themselves. And then Soluso said, 'Three, and that includes the boy. There used to be seven. Apart from the girl, three have died in the last four years.'

'Go into the village and do as you have said,' I spoke in a grim voice, my eyes staring into space, my mind spinning.'

'I was waiting for you to come,' the Chief said, when I got to the palace. 'I heard what happened.' He sighed and bowed his head, massaging his temples slowly with his fingers. And, to my surprise, he took off his crown.

In those days, when a chief took off his crown in the presence of anyone, a woman especially, it meant that he was grieved in his spirit and ready to take an action that could portend life or death, or one of revolutionary consequence.

He held his crown in his hand for a while, still with his head bowed. When he looked up, he spoke with a powerful voice, the voice of a chief. 'What do you want me to do for you?' he asked, putting his crown back on.

'Another orphan must not die in this village. There are three of them left. I want to turn my home into an orphanage. I want to take them in.'

'The priests will fight against it. Some of the people will fight against it too. Are you ready for what may come?'

'Yes, I'm ready, your majesty. I have those who will support me. In the end, I'm sure that I will have more supporters than opponents. I'm ready to make my case before the priests and the whole village.' My voice was grim.

He leaned forward and spoke in that conspiratorial tone that I had come to know. 'Remember, the more people you have on your side, the better your chances against the priests. You know you have my support. That should give you some motivation. There is no time to waste. This has become a community emergency. As you have said, another orphan must not die. I will call a meeting in two days' time. Then, you can make your case.'

'Thank you, your majesty,' I said with a bow.

He hardened his jaw briefly. And then in a soft tone, he asked, 'How is your son taking the shock?'

'He is taking it well,' I said. 'I have given him the secret of happiness, so he is never sad.'

The Chief's eyes widened. 'You know the secret of happiness?' he asked.

'Yes, your majesty.'

'Could you give me that secret when this matter has been resolved?'

'Yes, Chief, I could.'

'I will call the meeting in two days' time. Prepare yourself.'

After I had gone, town criers went round the village to announce the forthcoming meeting.

That night I called a meeting of my own, after Noah had gone to bed. Oyi, Soluso, Kewe, Chamuke and all the men and women who had worked in the house since the days of Mama gathered in the living room, and Soluso spoke first.

'Those of us who worked for Mama knew her dream,' he began. 'She told us that you would be coming long before you came, and it happened exactly as she had said. And she also told us that one day her house would become a place of refuge for orphans. We believe that this too will come to pass, exactly as she said. Mama was a kind woman. In you, we see her, and we are prepared to support you in every way possible to realise her dream. We have discussed this carefully amongst ourselves, and we believe that you came to accomplish that which Mama could not.' He stopped and turned to Kewe.

'All the young people are behind you,' Kewe said. 'We have decided that enough is enough. We will no longer watch poor children die while the aged continue to walk about bent over with bitterness and walking with sticks. At the meeting at the palace, we will show our support for you.'

Everyone nodded.

'I want to know the names and ages of the other orphans,' I said.

'Kenuli is a ten-year-old boy; Oma a seven-year-old girl; and there is Bobo, who is about nine,' Soluso explained.

'The Chief has promised to allow me to address the priests and the entire village and make my case for why I should be allowed to take the orphans into my care. I will appeal to the sensibility of the people. In the end, my case may be strengthened or weakened by the amount of support I get from the people. So you must all do your best to win as much support as possible for this cause. I will be counting on you.'

They nodded.

'You must be strong,' Kewe said. 'The priests will throw everything at you. They will threaten you with blindness and madness and death for taking the position you have. You have to be strong. Don't let their words weaken your heart. You're fighting for a good cause. We will support you steadfastly and you will get victory in the end.'

By the time we brought the meeting to a close, I could hear the silent cries of children in the night. I knew that I must be strong.

16

The amount of dust in the air indicated that the entire village had gathered at the palace. For a long time, everyone spoke at the same time. The sun burnt harshly while we waited for the Chief to come out. When he finally did, he came alone, without bodyguards.

Absolute silence fell. And then he greeted the crowd with a powerful voice. The response was resounding but solemn. He did not bother to sit on the stool that had been placed on the balcony for his use. Instead, he paced the balcony and began to address the village. 'I thank you all for coming,' he said. 'And now I will request that the priests come up to the balcony.'

Seven priests filed up the balcony from the front row where they had been standing. Their faces were severe. They stood, three on either side of the High Priest, and they chewed their lips quietly, their eyes fixed upon the crowd. Only the High Priest carried a short broom and he was dressed in the same fashion as the day he had paid me a visit. The others were dressed in long white robes, and each carried a gourd which looked like a horn. You could tell that they were ready to invoke the gods. My heart began to beat fearfully.

Again, the Chief spoke. 'May I request that Ese come up to the balcony, also. This meeting has much to do with her.'

For a few moments I was rooted to a spot, too afraid to take a step out of the crowd. And then Kewe nudged me. 'Go out,' he whispered. 'Be strong, you have our support.'

Noah looked up at me. I patted him on the head and walked up to the balcony on wobbly legs. I stood to the left of the Chief. And, focusing my eyes on Noah, who smiled encouragingly at me, I suddenly received strength. I took a deep breath. I turned to look at the Chief. I did not bother to look at the priests, who were standing to his far right. The Chief acknowledged me with a slight nod of his head.

'An orphan girl died yesterday,' the Chief continued. 'She had gone with her brother to Ese's house. The uncle punished them for going, and unfortunately the girl died. But the uncle cannot be held responsible for the girl's death. Our laws protect him.' He paused. 'The incident would have ended like that whoever the orphan's relative had been. But yesterday, Ese visited me and said that she would like to turn her home into an orphanage and take in every orphan.

'As you all know, I do not make laws. Our laws are made by the priests. And it is up to the people to accept or reject them. And as you all know, Ese is one of us. Mama told us of her coming long before she came, so she's Mama's daughter and therefore entitled to enjoy every right as a citizen of our village. So, she will be given the opportunity to make her case before all of us. And it is up to you, the people, to support or oppose her.

'In the event that she gets the majority of your support, then the priests will have to review the law in question, subject to my approval, of course. But if she fails to get majority support, then the priests will invoke the punishment of the gods upon her.

'I must point out, even if she gets your support, and I recommend that the law be reviewed, the priests could still invoke the punishment of the gods, but she would be free to do as she pleases. And it would be up to the gods to either punish or exonerate her. So, by the power bestowed upon me, I call upon Ese to open her case.'

* * *

For a moment, all was still.

I kept my eyes intently on Noah. It was all

that I needed to do to sustain my courage. And then I spoke. 'Your majesty, I greet you. Great priests, I greet you. Good people of our village, I greet you too. I'm most grateful for the opportunity given to me to address this gathering.' I paused. 'I was afraid before I climbed this balcony. But I saw my son in the crowd smiling at me, and I became strong. I became strong because of my son. He is a happy boy. He reminds me that every child deserves to be happy. That's why I believe that the law which condemns orphans should be abolished.'

There were gasps of shock from the priests.

I continued. 'Not only would I like to see the law abolished, I would also like to convert my house into an orphanage. Since orphans are not shown the love they deserve by their relatives, I would like to take them in and care for them. I . . . '

The Chief raised a hand to stop me. 'You have opened your case. The High Priest will come forward to respond, and then you will get the opportunity to make your submission,' he said and motioned in the direction of the priests.

The High Priest strode forward, tall and imposing. He did not bother to observe formalities. His chest pumping and his eyes flaming with fire, he spoke in a thunderous voice. 'We must not bring the wrath of the gods upon ourselves by breaking the laws they gave us.' He paused to survey the crowd. 'None in this village has ever disobeyed the gods, and I'm sure none will dare to do so now. Let us not forget, the gods speak in many ways. They could bring down heavy rain to punish us. And they could send thunder and lightning to destroy us.'

Even as he spoke, the clouds suddenly darkened and a growl of thunder shook the sky. He continued. 'It's clear that the gods are speaking even now. If you choose to support Ese, be aware that great disaster will surely come upon this land. Don't bring sickness and disease upon yourselves. Do not say I didn't warn you.' With these words, he stepped back and joined the other priests.

A much louder growl followed in the wake of his words. And then the people began to debate fiercely amongst themselves. I sensed that a great fear had come upon them. I looked on desperately, wondering if they would be bold enough to give me their support now. I could see Kewe and Soluso, heads together, discussing in an agitated manner.

The Chief took over. He looked round at the crowd, and then he asked, 'Do you, the people, support Ese?'

There was no response. A lengthy and much louder growl shook the sky.

The Chief asked the question again. This time, only the isolated voices of Kewe, Soluso and Oyi could be heard. My heart began to pound painfully in my chest. The High Priest had succeeded in putting fear in the people. I had lost. I wondered what would happen to Bobo and the other orphans. I blamed myself for Ada's death, and for condemning her brother to a life of suffering. Tears of frustration welled up in me. I became too sad to focus my eyes on Noah.

For a moment all was quiet. The Chief was about to speak again when a car suddenly appeared in a cloud of dust in the distance. As far as I knew, it was the first time a car had come to the village. The sound of the approaching car caused the crowd to turn round, and shouts of surprise rose into the air. Even the priests had started to talk in excited voices amongst themselves. I turned to look at the Chief. His face was placid as he watched the approaching vehicle. With the proceedings now disrupted, he raised his voice in, 'We will wait to see who the visitor is before we continue with this meeting.' He signalled to some of his guards standing on the front row, instructing them to go and welcome the visitor and bring him to the balcony.

★ ★ ★

In the commotion that had ensued, I could no longer see Noah, Oyi and the others from where I stood on the balcony. The dust was thicker than ever and they had been swallowed up by the confusion. My heart began to beat with fear. I thought of going to look for Noah, but with the Chief and the priests still on the balcony, I could not leave. I prayed that Oyi would hold tightly on to him.

The car had parked by now. Before long, the guards brought the visitor to the balcony. He was a tall, slim man in his early sixties. He wore a benign smile and he carried himself with dignity. He bowed briefly to greet the Chief. Then he looked round and nodded to all.

The crowd pushed forward, eager to get a closer view of the visitor, to know who he was. Where he had parked his car, several kids had gathered around it. Some guards struggled to disperse them.

The dark clouds had started to clear now, and a lengthy growl in the sky finally died down, indicating that the rain had blown away. The Chief called for silence. 'We have a visitor in our midst,' he said. 'First we will welcome him and ask him to introduce himself, and then we will continue with our meeting. He turned to the visitor. 'On behalf of the entire village, I welcome you. I hope you have come in peace.'

'Thank you, your majesty,' the man replied. 'I'm from the city and I come in peace.' He spoke in a quiet and cultured voice.

'May I ask you to speak as loud as possible for the benefit of the people?' the Chief said, politely. 'What brings you to our village?'

'I'm a son of this soil,' the man replied. 'I have come back to my roots.'

Loud cries of disbelief went up in the air. The priests gathered their heads together, whispering anxiously.

'You mean you're a son of this village?' the Chief asked, in a toneless voice. 'Please explain.'

'My name is Professor Andu Abibe,' he said, 'Prof, as they would call me in the city. I'm a retired lecturer. As I said, I come from this village, but I doubt if any among you would remember me. I left when I was barely ten. In fact, I ran away, as an orphan, because I was subjected to unthinkable torture. I went first to the town, and then to the city where I met a good man, who took me in and gave me education. I came to know him as father. He had a good wife, who accepted me as her son.

'Although they have both passed away, their blessed memories continue to live with me. I lived and got education in the city, and I have even travelled to the white man's land a few times. I have seen the ends of the world. But now I have come back to my roots to share the love and knowledge I have learnt on my journeys. This is the summary of my story.'

The crowd had become absolutely quiet while he spoke. Even the priests had stopped whispering amongst themselves as they listened raptly to him. The dust had settled, and a lengthy silence passed after he finished speaking. I watched the man with fascination. I wanted to go before him and welcome him and ask someone to fetch him water to drink. But I was simply transfixed. All I could hear were his words, as they continued to echo in my ears.

★ ★ ★

Finally, the crowd stirred, and excited voices filled the air once again. It was beyond belief that an orphan who ran away from the village had become a prosperous lecturer in the city and returned with a car. And he said that he had even travelled to the white man's land! I just stared at the man in astonishment. 'You're welcome back to your roots,' I heard the Chief saying to him. 'A meeting was ongoing when you arrived. Since you're a son of our soil, you have the right to be a part of this meeting. So we shall continue.' He turned to me, 'Ese, the people have not shown you much support so far. Now you must step forward and put up your closing arguments.'

I looked at the Chief and then at the Professor. I faced the crowd. I could see Noah now, standing beside Oyi. I could see Kewe and Soluso. I thought of Ada, Bobo and the other orphans. I took a deep breath and then I began to build my case all over again, for the benefit of Prof, and the people too, considering that a man who was once an orphan had come to share a story of hope with us.

By the time I finished speaking, not a sound could be heard. It was as if the people were afraid even to breathe. I turned to look at the Chief. His jaw was set. And then he spoke.

'Again I ask you, the people,' he said, 'do you support Ese?'

There was no response.

'Are you against Ese?'

Still no response.

He tried again. 'Ese has presented her case. Are you in support of her?'

A solitary voice said, 'Yes.' And immediately, there was a deafening roar of 'Yes!'

The Chief asked a second time to be sure. The support from the crowd was louder than before. He turned to the priests. 'You may now speak,' he said.

The High Priest stepped forward. He spoke in a very loud voice filled with anger. 'All our laws were given to us by the gods,' he began. 'And they also set the punishments to be pronounced on law-breakers.' He paused. 'We all know that the punishment for breaking the laws of the god is blindness, madness and then death. It would be pure foolishness for anyone to bring these terrible punishments on themselves. Since Ese has chosen to oppose the gods, I have no option but to pronounce judgment on her.

'If she goes ahead with her plans now that you, the people, have given her your support, and that the Chief may ask for a review of the law in question, I pronounce, in the name of the gods of our land, that within seven days she will go blind, run mad and die!' He held his broom firmly in the air as he spoke, and his words came out with chilling potency.

'These are the words of the gods, not of man, they shall come to pass.' For a moment, he trembled hypnotically from head to toe, and then he stepped back and joined his fellow priests.

The crowd broke out in loud voices, as if a great confusion had come upon them, or as if they were about to witness something they had never witnessed before. It was the first time anyone had challenged the priests and the first time anyone had gone up against the gods.

★   ★   ★

The Chief turned to me. 'Ese, the High Priest has spoken,' he said. 'Do you want to go ahead? Are you ready for the consequences that may come?'

I look from the Chief to the Professor and then the crowd. Prof smiled at me encouragingly. In the crowd, Noah fixed his eyes upon me in anticipation. 'Yes, your majesty,' I said, 'I'm prepared to go ahead.'

'In that case, I proclaim that you may take every orphan into your home. And I hereby abolish the law that condemns them,' he said.

The crowd roared. The dust in the air thickened. The Chief raised his hand and asked for silence. It took several minutes for quiet to prevail. When he had gained their attention, he announced, 'You may now go back to your homes.'

The crowd began to disperse, amidst a babble of talk. The Chief turned to Prof and welcomed him warmly again. And then he took me aside, and he bent down to whisper in my ear. 'I told you I would conspire with you, remember?' He did not wait to get a response from me. He continued: 'I arranged for Prof to come from the city. I met him when I lived there. He told me his story, that he was from our village and that he would love to return to his roots one day. Yesterday, I sent an urgent message to him, that it was time for him to come back.'

I was too stunned to say a word.

He turned abruptly away from me. The priests were waiting to consult him.

17

That very day, Enforcers from the palace went to collect the three orphans from the homes of their relatives. The household staff, Noah and I welcomed them with great rejoicing, but they looked cold and frightened. Bobo would not stop weeping, and he kept repeating the words, 'my sister'. I held him to me, consoling him, telling him that his sister had gone to a better place, that he was safe now. But he looked at me with tears in his eyes and asked if he could join his sister where she had gone. I could not answer his question. I just held him to me, whispering quiet words into his hair, holding back my own tears with all the willpower I could muster.

While Noah took Bobo to his room, I introduced myself to Oma and Kenuli, the older orphans, both of whom the staff had been fawning over. I hugged them and told them that they were in their new home now. They looked at each other, uncertainty in their eyes. And then Oma gave a quiet hiss and shrugged, as if resigned to whatever may come. She wiped her tired face with her palm, sighed and folded her arms across her chest. She looked very thin with scars all over her body, and she wore an anxious look as if she was going to burst into tears any minute. 'Why are we here?' she asked, as if expecting me to begin to load them with punishments and assignments.

'This is your new home now,' I said, pulling her to me. 'You will live here with me from now on and I will take good care of you, Kenuli and Bobo.' I pulled Kenuli to me with one hand. 'My son Noah will be your brother. All of us will live happily together forever.'

'Who are you?' she asked, uncertainly.

'Call me auntie Ese. I'm auntie to both of you now, and to Bobo too,' I said. And I introduced to them the staff who had been lingering in the corner of the room. The orphans merely looked round at everyone suspiciously, saying nothing.

Kenuli seemed to be taciturn. His eyes were wide. I suspected that he had developed this feature over time, as a result of all the hardship he had endured. He looked very strong, like a boy who had conditioned himself to suffering, who expected nothing in life but suffering. I reached out and touched his face gently, allowing my palm to linger upon his cheek. 'I'm your auntie now,' I told him. 'You don't have to be afraid anymore.'

He heaved a couple of anxious breaths, like one who had been crying for a long time as a result of a painful injustice that he had suffered. I placed my palm on his chest.

Oyi walked in with steaming dishes of food on a wooden tray.

'And that is auntie Oyi,' I said to them. 'She's one of the good people who will be looking after you from now.' And with excitement in my voice, I announced, 'And now it's time to eat! Afterwards, you will take a bath and I will show you to your rooms.'

They exchanged looks. I led them to the dining table while Oyi went to get Noah and Bobo. Noah had managed to pacify Bobo. He no longer had tears in his eyes, but he wore an expectant look, as if waiting for something bad to happen or to wake up from a dream.

More trays of food were brought in by the staff and we all sat at the table, and as we were about to begin to eat, a knock came on the gate. Soluso went to see who it was. Soon he returned with Prof.

We all scrambled to our feet to greet him. He smiled benignly at us. His presence seemed to fill the room with calm. 'I see you're about to eat,' he said.

'Yes,' I replied. 'Please join us.' I felt so glad that he had come.

Quickly, Oyi and I created space for him at the table.

'Thank you for sharing your food with me,' he said as he took his seat. 'I will have just a little as I have already eaten.'

We all fixed our eyes on him. In our tradition, the eldest person at the table helped themselves first, and then others followed.

Instead of washing his hands in the bowl of water that had been provided for him, he bowed his head and spread out his hands. We watched him. We did not know what he was doing. He said to Soluso, who was to his right, 'Take my hand.' Soluso took his hand. And he said to Noah, who was to his left, 'Take my hand.' Noah copied Soluso. He looked round at the rest of us. 'Take the hand of the person to your left and to your right.

We obeyed silently.

'Let's bow our heads and share the grace,' he said.

We imitated him, looking up at him curiously with our eyes open.

'We thank you, Lord for the food that we're about to share. Bless this food, Oh Lord. Amen!'

And then he began to eat. The rest of us followed suit.

★ ★ ★

After we had finished eating we sat out in the yard, with two lanterns burning. Oyi and some of the other staff had gone to draw bathing water for the children. I sat with Prof and Soluso. Up in the sky the stars were out, in their brilliant millions, and the chirp of insects punctuated the stillness of the night.

'Thank you for coming to visit us,' I said to Prof.

'I'm glad that I came, and I'm glad that I met a strong girl like you.' He sat up and stretched his legs. We stayed in silence for a few moments. And then he asked, 'Are you worried about the curse the priest pronounced on you?'

I thought about his question. I shook my head. 'I don't really care,' I said. 'I believe that I will be making a big difference if I could care for those poor children for just one day. And that's all that matters to me. I do not care what happens to me after that.'

'I'm glad I met you,' he said once again, nodding his head. 'You see, the gods the priests claim to serve are powerless.'

Soluso caught his breath sharply.

Prof continued. 'The gods they claim to worship are a creation of their evil minds, which they use to put fear in people in order to control them. Such gods do not exist. And the laws they make are the wicked lies of a very ignorant people. I was an orphan, they labelled me an evil child with their laws, but here I'm today. I met a good man and his good wife who cared for me and gave me a future. And because of the love they showed me I have been able to see the ends of the world. There's a God up in heaven to whom all power belongs. He is not a God you can access through tradition or religion, but through love. And it's that love that is lacking in the hearts of the priests and all who uphold their laws.

'Fear not. No evil shall befall you. The curse pronounced on you by the priests shall come to nought. They have given you seven days to live. You will live far beyond that time, and everyone will come to see how powerless their gods are. What this village needs is good education for the children for they're the custodian of the future. I will work with you to provide education not only for the children in your care, but for all children. And one day, the evil traditions of this and other villages will be wiped out.'

★ ★ ★

I wondered if I was in a dream, if all of this was really happening. For a while, I feared that I might wake up to find it all a cruel joke.

But Prof's voice affirmed the authenticity of things and the great possibilities of the future.

'Tell us about yourself,' I said, 'about your family in the city.' As I asked this question, my mind went to Kpofe, and for a moment, I prayed that he was okay, that things had gotten better for him.

'There's nothing to tell about me, nothing to tell about you or any of us who are grown enough to be called adults,' Prof said. 'All there is to tell is about the children of our society whom we owe a sacred duty. And the duty we owe them means that we must guide them correctly and provide them good education that will open their minds to the greatest possibilities. So there's really nothing to tell about me. And, I already know all that I need to know about you, that you're a very kind and courageous woman. These are the qualities you need to make a difference in society.'

Soluso and I were subdued by the profoundness of his words. I wished I could just sit there and listen to him forever. I knew Soluso felt the same way.

When they had finished taking their baths, the children came to join us. I felt glad to see that they were all in much better moods. They were warmly clothed to protect them from the night's chill. I felt glad to see the way they walked towards us, together, like loving siblings.

'Come and sit beside me,' Prof said, motioning them over. He got them to sit two on either side of him. He asked them their names and chatted with them. He said jokes that made them laugh. It felt really nice to see them laugh. Kenuli spoke quietly. Oma laughed the most, as if she had suddenly found invaluable happiness. And then Bobo asked, 'Has my sister really gone to a better place?'

Prof already knew his story. 'Yes, your sister has gone to a better place,' he said. 'And if you behave well, you will go there too one day. Okay?'

The boy nodded.

'Before you go to bed, let me tell you this,' Prof said in a quiet voice. 'I was once an orphan in this village. And then I travelled to the city and I met a good man and his good wife who took me in and cared for me. The love they showed me made me who I am today. I have come to share that love with you. One day you too will share it with others and you will be very happy.'

'I know the secret of happiness,' Noah said, eagerly.

'You know?' Prof asked.

'Yes, Mother told me the secret of

happiness,' he said.

'And what is it?' Prof asked.

'The secret of happiness is that we must be happy at all times, even if the whole world is sad.'

'Beautiful!' Prof exclaimed. 'And that's what each of you must always do. You must always be happy at all times, even if the whole world is sad. Okay?' He bent down to look at their faces.

They nodded.

'Good. Now it's time for you to go to bed.'

★   ★   ★

Kewe and Chamuke arrived shortly after the children had gone to their rooms. They were delighted to meet Prof, who welcomed them warmly. Sitting round the two lanterns, we chatted late into the night. Prof did not tell us anything about himself, but he spoke about his plans to give education to the children of the village.

'It's a good thing that you're starting off with an orphanage,' he said. 'It provides me the platform to bring them education. Gradually, we could attract other children and build a proper school for the entire village.'

'I like your plan,' I said. 'This house is very

big, we could convert a part of it into a school.'

'One room would do, if you would be kind enough to allow me to use it as a classroom.'

'Of course,' I replied. 'I went to the town the other day with Oyi, and we saw children in uniform coming from school. And I thought that it was possible for us to have a school in the village too. It is amazing that you have come to make that dream a reality.'

'I saw it as a wild dream that day you mentioned it,' Oyi said.

'Everything starts with a dream,' Prof said.

'I agree,' Oyi said.

Finally, Prof rose to his feet. 'I have to return to the palace,' he said. 'The Chief was kind enough to provide me lodgings. I must go back before it gets too late.'

We all rose. I wished he did not have to go.

★　★　★

I took the decision to shut the shop temporarily to give me the chance to attend to the children, and to fine-tune plans for the school with Prof. He came every day, his presence was uplifting for everyone. The children liked to gather around him. They liked his jokes because it made them laugh.

Bobo was gradually overcoming his sister's

death. But you could tell that he thought about her now and then. Kenuli was becoming chattier, but his eyes remained wide, betraying the fear he had lived with most of his life. I hoped that time would heal his wound, that the wideness of his eyes would become one of joy and delight. Oma was like a child who having suddenly discovered happiness could no longer remain silent or still. She pranced around the house, and she talked and laughed more than everyone. It was a great credit to Noah, who was always sharing the secret of happiness with them, so that in spite of all the pain and sadness they had been through, they were able to exude a happiness that thrilled the rest of us.

Seven days after the meeting at the palace, I had not gone blind or run mad. And I was still alive. On the eighth day, most of the villagers gathered in front of my house, to know what had become of me. The fact that the shop remained closed heightened their curiosity. But when they saw me going and coming, walking without a cane to guide me, still fully clothed and not raving-naked mad, they talked with great excitement amongst themselves.

On the twelfth day I went with the children to the palace to greet the Chief. A large crowd followed us as we went. The Chief had been notified of our coming. He came out to welcome us, smiling, triumphant, holding his royal staff high up in the air.

'Ese, I can see that you're well and alive,' he said in a loud voice. 'And that your children are doing well, too.'

'Yes, your majesty,' I replied.

The crowd behind us gave a jubilant shout that shook the world.

The next day, the priests gathered their families and left the village quietly, paving the way for a new dawn.

★ ★ ★

One evening, a week later, my heart led me to The Gate. I sat on Mama's rock, alone, thinking of all that had happened in so short a time. I wondered which village the priests and their families had moved to. I felt certain that they would never again be able to sow lies.

I waited. I did not know what I was waiting for. But I did not have long to wait. My eyes were fixed on the rock on which I was seated. When I looked up, I saw him coming from afar. He had a bag across his shoulder. Even before I could make out his face I knew it was him. Kpofe. My heart began to beat with joy, and I mouthed a thank-you to Bisco.

I got to my feet and we ran towards each other. And when we embraced, I thought my heart would burst from my chest. We gazed deeply into each other's eyes. 'I'm so glad you came,' I said.

He smiled. He looked very well; and colourful as usual. I felt grateful that the city had not beaten him.

'When Bisco told me he had found you, I knew I had to come,' he said. 'Let's sit down, we need to talk. And please don't say anything until I finish.'

I led him to Mama's rock, and we sat down side by side. He dropped his bag and took my hand. 'You have survived the worst, and I'm very glad for you,' he said. 'I went to the village after you ran away and I was told all that happened. You must put the past behind you. And that's why I have come. As I have said, you have survived the worst. Do not be afraid to face the future.'

He paused, then continued. 'Bisco told me you live in this village with your son now.' He squeezed my hand. 'Ese, it is true that Noah died when you went in search of Mazamaza. And he was buried before you got back. The boy that now lives with you is not Noah.'

'But he is Noah,' I said in alarm. 'You will see for yourself, he is Noah, except that he no longer has the birthmark on his back.'

He smiled gently. 'He is a gift given to you to replace the son you lost, because you have shown so much faith, because you believed so fiercely that your son did not die. I cannot lie to you, Ese. I was told what happened in the village. Noah is dead.'

For a long moment we were silent. I thought about the missing birthmark, and I nodded my head in understanding. Tears welled in my eyes. Kpofe pulled me to him and wiped my tears. 'Don't cry,' he said. 'The boy is indeed your son now, your gift. Only you and I know this. You have a future ahead of you, and I have come to share it with you. Please don't cry.'

I smiled at him. Then I looked out along the road. It had brought me my last gift. All the years I had spent searching for love had brought me to this spot, the end of the road, where I would find it.

I had reached my destination, my destiny, my place, yet still, an eternity remained ahead. One filled with love, faith and freedom.

Epilogue

Many suns passed and moons came and went.

Noah had grown into a strong man. At twenty-three, he had acquired education, travelled to the towns and city, and seen a bit of the world. And then one evening at dinner, he cleared his throat and announced to us, 'I'm going to visit the village of Mother's stories.'

'Go, come back and tell us about your journey,' I said to him with a smile.

He took off the following morning, in a car similar to the one that Prof had driven from the city all those years ago. When he came back a few days later he had an incredible story to tell.

The journey that had taken me one month on foot took him only a few hours. The world had changed, civilisation had advanced, and distance had been bridged.

He arrived in the outskirts of the village as a heavy downpour began. He saw an abandoned building, and he decided to take shelter there until the rain stopped because visibility had become poor and the road treacherous. He was surprised to find a couple of young boys in the building, lying on the floor of the living room.

He apologised for intruding and asked if the building was their home. They explained to him that they had no home; that it was a place of temporary shelter for them until they were able to leave the village and go to a place where nobody knew them. They told him they were orphans, and, suddenly, he recollected the building from the stories I had told him.

He spoke with the children, and with their permission he took a walk through the rooms to see what the place looked like. It was just as he had always imagined it, just as I had described.

In a room filled with old boxes and piles of junk, which the boys explained they never used, he lingered.

As he walked through the room, his foot kicked against a board protruding from under a pile of rubbish and he almost fell. He pulled out the offending piece of board to put it away safely, but to his surprise he discovered that it was not a board at all, but a painting of many colours. He removed years of dust with his hands.

He did not need to look too closely before realising that it was *Ese*, the painting about which I had told him so much. He held it up to the light by a window. He was amazed to see me standing in the middle of a market, exactly as I had told him. In the background, he saw the indistinct face of a handsome young man. For a few moments, he just stared at the face. And then it suddenly occurred to him that it was his own face staring back. He began to tremble with wonder.

He gathered from the boys that there had been a great famine in the land for years. When the rain stopped, he told them to wait for him, that he would be back soon. He left his car behind to show them that he would honour his word. He carried the painting under one arm and completed the journey to the village on foot.

The people had been waiting for him for so long. They gathered around him to admire the painting, and they told him about the prophecy made by a High Priest a long time ago. They said he was the Chief that would lead them into an era of prosperity, and they begged him to dwell amongst them.

But he told them that he must settle something first. So he came back to tell me what had happened, and that he felt in his bones that becoming their Chief was what he was meant to do.

I helped him to pack. A few days later, I drove with him in his car to The Gate. 'Go and pursue your destiny, my son,' I said, leaning across to hug him. Then I climbed out of the car and set my eyes upon the road that would lead my son to his destiny.

For a long time after he had driven out of my sight, I continued to look out along the road, with a smile on my face.

Acknowledgements

After finishing my first book, I had a Skype conference with my then editor Louisa Joyner and my agent Toby Mundy to discuss book two. I put forward three ideas, and Louisa suggested that I work on this particular story as against the one I favoured. I have not stopped admiring her for her prescience since. Alas she moved on and handed me to my new editor, Joanna Dingley. This is how I came to be so fortunate to be guided by two elegantly creative editors. A big thank-you to Louisa Joyner and to Joanna Dingley. You are great blessings to my writing.

A few chapters into the writing of this book, plagued by doubts, I turned to the man who showed me the way in the beginning. He offered me invaluable suggestions and encouragement. Trevor Dolby, a big thank-you.

To my agent Toby Mundy, who helped me to discover what he calls 'the song in my voice', I can never express my gratitude enough. Your contribution in the writing of this book and to shaping my career is invaluable.

I say a big thank-you to 'The Big Man' Jamie Byng and all the good folks at Canongate; to my German publisher Ulrike Ostermeyer and all on the Ark; to everyone at Random House US; to all at Yurt Kitap Yayin, for refusing to be intimidated by barrel and boot; to all at Frassinelli; to Clare Christian, who has been there from the beginning; to my brilliant copy editor Alison Rae; and to all who helped in numerous ways. To the Creator, who wrote this story through me, I owe my deepest gratitude.